More Aster(ix) Anthologies

10th Anniversary Issue: Part I - Poetry & Nonfiction
Spring 2023

The Tarot Issue
December 2022

Mothers Unearthed
September 2022

Winter Fiction
December 2021

Best of Hot Metal Bridge
April 2021

The Ferrante Project
October 2020

The Poetry Issue
Winter 2020

Inheritance
Summer 2019

(Un)bound [double issue]
Winter 2018/2019

and more!

available for order wherever books are sold

and don't forget to visit
asterixjournal.com
for more content and information

Aster(ix) Journal
www.asterixjournal.com

Aster(ix) print issues are usually published twice a year with additional content online. **Aster(ix)** is funded in part by the Dietrich School of Arts and Sciences and the Department of English at University of Pittsburgh.

Aster(ix) Journal

presents

10th Anniversary Issue

Part II: Fiction & Interviews

Edited by
Angie Cruz

December 2023

BLUE SKETCH PRESS | PITTSBURGH

Individual acknowledgments available on pg. [TK]
Published via Blue Sketch Press, Pittsburgh.
www.bluesketchpress.com

10th Anniversary Issue: Part II
An Aster(ix) Anthology / Aster(ix) Journal
Edited by Angie Cruz—1st ed.

ISBN (print) 978-1-942547-21-1 (trade paperback)
942547211X (ISBN-10)

Cover art by Karla Caloca
Cover Design by Little Owl Creative

First Edition: December 2023

Printed in the United States of America
9 8 7 6 5 4 3 2 1

Contents

LETTER FROM THE EDITOR

Angie Cruz

Dear ones,

We are thrilled to share the second part of our tenth anniversary double issue, highlighting some of the best short fiction and interviews our journal has to offer.

Thank you to everyone who has stepped in, stepped up, volunteered their time, trusted us with their contributions, accepted our invitations, invited yourselves to the party, forgave us when we didn't respond, and asked time and time again: "How can we help?" Who said, "If we can help, we will."Thank you to each and every one of you who makes up this brilliant collective of writers, artists, editors, readers, and community members that we call la Aster(ix) familia.

We have arrived to ten years because we have each other. Aster(ix) was born as a place of play, a laboratory, a publication that invites writers to take their time with their work. It is the censored and omitted. It is footnotes and to be continued. Aster(ix) honors Mayan heart knowing, the alignment with divine will, the torchbearer. We continue to cast lines between the future and the past, the possible and the impossible.

Pa'lante,
Angie

Originally published in our Fall 2017 issue, *Dirty Laundry*

Drawing Maps

Sandra Cisneros with Angie Cruz

We began our conversation with Sandra Cisneros drawing our own personal maps of the United States. Drawing jump-started our conversation about latinidad, place, writing, privilege, power, and activism. In the end we journeyed together in conversation remembering and thinking through how we work and continue to work as Latina/o creatives and scholars. Also in attendance: Angie Cruz, Clarissa A. León, Armando García, Adriana E. Ramírez, Elizabeth Rodriguez Fielder, Tanya Shirazi and Angela Velez.

Angie Cruz: One of the reasons we started Aster(ix) was in response to the question, who is publishing women writers of color? Through my work with the journal I've realized how many writers of color, even the more established writers, are having a difficult time placing their work, especially when the work is not performing their identity politics. But also we have found that women of color don't always submit their work. They need to be solicited.

Sandra Cisneros: I don't send my poems out unless someone asks me.

AC: Me neither, and this is true for many women writers I know. So then people are like, what happened to her? Is she publishing? That's one of the reasons we started Aster(ix). To find each other. To put our works in conversation with each other.

AC: A lot of writers that I know, especially those that are sending their work out, feel if their work doesn't legibly appear to be Latino/a—it has a more difficult time getting placed. What do you think?

Adriana E. Ramírez: I think it's less so in nonfiction.

AC: But what Latino/a in nonfiction that is published isn't writing about a Latin-American/ latino/a problem?

AER: It depends on who you are. If a Latino/a historian is writing about the history of the Apache, I don't think that's necessarily performing your identity. I think it's a unique perspective of a historical thing. I can't divorce myself from who I am. I look in the mirror and see the nopal and everything. You are who you are. Even the way I use language, the aphorisms that pop up. Even "Cero a la izquierda," doesn't even sound right in English. "Zeros to the left"?

AC: I do think the dearth of Latina writers getting published each year makes creating spaces such as Macondo and Aster(ix) an urgent matter, even if neither of our activist efforts are by no means exclusively Latino/a. What I also realized is how many writers, because they are activists, mothers, etc., don't have the time and space to write. I think we desperately need writing residencies, where we're asked to do nothing but our creative work.

SC: But don't you think too that some part of not making the time to write is also that we make ourselves too available? Regarding activism, I think when we rescue, it's because we're rescuing some part of ourselves too. That's what a therapist would tell you. You're rescuing, but you're rescuing yourself too. Where you don't feel you do enough, or you feel guilty because of your success or whatever it is. That's why I started the foundation. I felt guilty there wasn't more success for others.

SC: Oh, I think we should do it, and then we should pass the baton. You don't have to do it your whole life or you don't have to do it for ten years. I think you can do it for as long as you can do it and once it had a good run somebody else can start something else. I often wonder if we make ourselves too available as women. We have to stop. I did two foundations, and I gave fifty fold. I don't have to feel like I'm a bad person now.

AC: Do any of you feel a pressure to be activists or give back? If so how?

Tanya Shirazi: I worked in educational outreach for eleven years before I finally decided to fully invest in my creative writing pursuit. I went to grad school in counseling. It was hard to leave those altruistic career spaces—I made close connections with first-generation Latinx undergrads. They are my second family. When I decided to pursue an MFA and leave I felt selfish. In my heart though, I knew it was time to nurture the creative part of me that I had ignored for so long. Sometimes we have to find a balance in how much we give to other people as well as to our craft.

SC: When Ursula K. Leguin turned 60, she went into sanctuary. She calls it sanctuary. She says I can't. I'm in sanctuary. And that's what you've got to say, 'I'm in sanctuary.' When I come out of sanctuary, you can approach me, but don't tell them when you're coming out of sanctuary. Never come out of sanctuary. You know, just go into sanctuary and say, 'Not now, I'm in sanctuary.'

AC: I love it. That's what I'm going to call it, my sanctuary. It's like what I used to tell my family when I moved back into my old neighborhood to get out of family commitments; I would say, 'Estoy estudiando.' 'Oh! Estudiando, esta bien!' 'Estudiando' was like the magical word. If I was studying, everyone left me alone.

* * *

AV: I think there can be many goals for something literary.

SC: I think publishers need to give young people the best. Because a young person may not read another book again. The difference between a good book and a great one is just time. Don't you think? And I think some writing needs another pasadita, another bit of editing. I think a lot of times writers, especially of color…is it Dr. Johnson who said, women writing, it's not that they write well but that they could write at all. Like a dog walking on its hind legs. Not that it walks well, but that it could walk at all. And I think sometimes editors treat Latino writers not that we can write well, but that we can write at all. And we should not lower ourselves to do work that isn't better than good and that's because people expect us to fail. I've always felt like people expect women and people of color to fail. So we got to do better than that.

AC: I do agree lots of works could use more time, but as an editor sometimes I get a story and give the writer feedback, and they will ignore my feedback, and publish it somewhere—and they are satisfied with just getting it published. And I say, why did they throw away that story? They've already spent a year on it, why not another week? So we are bombarded in general with such mediocrity. To me, publishing mediocre work is another form of pollution. Content pollution.

SC: They're not honoring their work.

AC: They could have given it another few months and try to take it to the next level, and it would have been better for their career in general.

SC: This is the thing that young writers don't realize. I'm on the panels giving them awards. I'm on those panels with the other judges that are looking at that manuscript and if you don't do a good job with that book it's going to hold you back from getting your next book, or getting an award. So every time you put a book out there that isn't your best, you're advertising that you're not the best. So, what do you want, the money? Or do you want to tell people you're a half-assed writer? Because that's what you're advertising.

AC: But also some writers never take the chance to put their work out. I find that sometimes I hold back, a kind of self censorship, or a thinking of an expectation of what I was supposed to be writing versus what I wanted to write. I always struggle with that. I guess it's because I'm one of the very few Dominicanas who has been published in English. But also I wasn't honoring how much I'd changed, and how much I'd grown from the books I had written. I have to trick myself to forget the audience and just write the book.

SC: I think you got to keep the audience out and when you're thinking about the audience is when you're either doing the small writing, the writing where you get your agenda out of the way. You have to work so hard to get your agenda out of the way.

AC: And I see so many writers of color that we solicit for Aster(ix) send us work, and I feel this tension in the work, where they are representing culture but also translating their experience to some general unknown audience that almost feels derivative of writing that they've read, or they think women of color should be writing. Writers—why are you writing about this? Is this really what you want to write about? But it's almost like, because that's all they've seen in the context of Latino/a narratives, they're stuck there. When I did research for Let It Rain Coffee, I was going to the archive in Santo Domingo to look at old newspapers and the archivist there said, don't make the same mistake that Vargas Llosa did with Feast of the Goat. And I said, What do you mean? "He wrote with his head. That's not our people!" He said that Llosa's book was very well researched but you can't feel anything. His advice: write from your heart.

SC: Yeah, yeah. That's the challenge. Edit with your head, but write from your heart. I used to tell people, turn this off, turn this on. When you write, write from here. (Taps chest) And then turn this off, and turn this on. (Taps head)

-

Editors' note: this interview has been condensed and edited for clarity. The entire original conversation is available to read online.

Appeared in our Spring 2017 Issue, *Best of Kweli*

Still Life

Cecca Austin Ochoa

I lie and say this scar's a gift from my cat. Three inches long, hypertrophic, silver and purple; it's like the hidden seam in taxidermy, only inside out. People look doubtful—including Ana who's got more scars than a lightning tree—but when they meet my cat, wild thing, they believe. She's feral with six toes, a clipped left ear and a face like a chupacabra. I put food out for her on the window sill when I hear her purring, then see those glowing lantern eyes in the night. She doesn't like to be touched. Only when she steps through the window onto the kitchen table and pushes her fanged face into my hand, do I run my fingers through her matted tabby coat. I click my tongue for her, my wild thing. She disappears for months at a time then suddenly shows up. She's like Ana in that way.

Ana was wild with excitement when she called me out of the blue, this after a year of giving me a cold shoulder. She told me she was engaged to Jake. Truth told, I'd been waiting for her to dump that fool. You see, Ana's my girl, somos guanaca-americanas. First generation Salvadoreñas born in the empire. I've known Ana since I was twelve years old. We met in the 90's in San Francisco, at a free summer day-camp—provided by the city to keep kids like us from spending our whole vacation on the couch in front of a TV. In my case, a plastic chair in a hospital lounge, waiting for Ma to finish her chemo treatments. At camp, a smiling woman with a long blonde braid, taught us how to draw dogs with #2 pencils: two ovals, a circle for the head, triangles for ears, a trapezoid nose, add the legs and a tail. I colored my dog pink and silver, Ana's had blood dripping from its mouth; we looked at each other and saw artists. By fall, we moved through the world like conjoined twins: Raquel and Ana, a four-armed two-headed beast tumbling down the halls of our Junior High School. We dressed in black, wore purple lipstick, got sugar high on gas station icees and scribbled *live wild and die free* on bus station shelters. I knew Ana like I knew myself.

Problem was, I knew Jake, too. Met him a few years ago, when he answered my ad: caramel skinned seductress, girlfriend experience. I waited for him on 43rd in my high-tops and cotton dress, surprised by his dopey smile. The springy way he walked in his leather oxfords as we passed the 90 cents a minute jack-off booths and the I <3 New York T-shirt shops, up to Martina's apartment. The apartment had a king-sized bed in the living room, a side table with vanilla scented candles and a glass vase filled with marbles, for the occasional rose. The deadbolt-locked bedroom door, where Martina lived hid behind a velvet curtain. Jake wanted me to spoon him, he wanted to brush my long black hair, he wanted to practice his Spanish pointing to different parts of my body with a crooked index finger. "Comeré el dedo," I said and bared my teeth. Then, he slapped me.

Flipping burgers. That's most of the guys I see. You want cheese on that? No one had slapped me before. Ears still ringing, I pulled my scalpel from under the pillow and growled, *leave now.* "Guess you don't like it rough," he said and put his hands up with a smirk. But I saw fear flash in his eyes; didn't take him long to get dressed. What would he know about what I like? I'm not in the business to make friends or get disrespected; I'm in it to pay the bills, and I won't see just anyone. There are women who will. One girl saw all the black-listed clients. She took pride in it, like she was tougher than the rest of us. She wore scarves to cover up the bruises around her neck, but she'd vanished. No one could find her and not because we hadn't looked.

That's how it is: People come and they go. Who knows where. I came to New York to work on my art, and 'cause Ana's here. Eventually, I'll live in the desert with solar panels and a house made from mud. Belong to no government, spend no money, make no profit for myself or anyone else. Una mujer salvaje. When I disappear, you'll never find me.

Not long after she'd broken up with Mauricio, Ana brought that baboso, Jake, to my group show in Chelsea. My piece Deer/man came from an ongoing series about the legacy of war, something we Salvadoreñas know a lot about. Ana's mother left El Salvador after her daughter, Ana's sister, was murdered and her husband disappeared by el escuadrón de la muerte. The death squads. Wiped off the face of the knowable earth.Deer/man had the head of a stag attached to a silicon torso of a man. The deer skin tapered into a v at the solar plexus. The hunted and the hunter stitched together. Deer/man protruded from a mirrored wall-mount shaped like a crest. I wanted people to see their expressions as they thought, poor deer.

While explaining my work in rogue taxidermy to another artist—how I take my scalpel and shave away bits of fat and sticky veins before rubbing salt into the hide; how I carefully diagram muscle structure before making a plaster cast—I saw Ana from across the gallery, and waved her over. Ana's beautiful: Full-lipped, gallon-sized breasts, wide hips, narrow but soft waist. A two-hourglass figure. She popped out of the crowd by my side, then Jake by hers.

When I saw him, my cheek burned and my mouth went dry, as though someone had stuffed a stocking down my throat. She introduced me and I smiled helplessly, thinking, of all the eight million people in New York, how the fuck did this creep sniff out my girl? Not to mention, I'd never told Ana how I butter my bread. She whispered in my ear, "He's the one," but I could barely hear over the sound of my heartbeat. I excused myself and turned back to the artist, loudly continuing to tell her how I dismember the cadavers, the difficulty of removing the cheeks. She patted my shoulder and headed to the bar.

"No, no," Ana was saying to Jake, as I turned back to them. "Raquel's sculptures are about embodiment. About historical memory."

"It's animal abuse," Jake said pushing his sorry hands into the pockets of his prep-school khaki's. He ignored me and stared at Ana with an expression like he'd hung a vacancy sign in the blue windows of his eyes.

I explained that factory farming was animal abuse. That I only used road kill. For conceptual and ethical reasons.

"Ethical?" he asked. "So, do you make enough money to support yourself with your art?"

My face flushed and I grabbed Ana's hand. "¿Como lo conociste?"

"The internets."

"He reminds me of Mauricio," I said. Ana dropped my hand and shot me a wounded look—those doll-eyes wide, lips parted like I'd stuck her with a knife. Two years later when I ran into her, after she'd married Jake, I'd remember that look. Betrayal. But, by then, she knew what she'd been stuck with.

If I'd been thinking clearly, I would have pulled the gag out that night in the Chelsea. I'd never told Ana about my work 'cause every time I thought about coming clean, I'd remember all the afternoons we spent side by side on the pink carpet of my Ma's living room floor pretending to do homework, but actually plotting our art world establishment takeover. She went on to work for an arts non- profit for the children of immigrants. I wanted her to think of me as the artist, not the puta. But I wasn't thinking clearly.

I called her up a few days later to apologize, knowing she'd be pissed I'd brought up Mauricio. Ana had been with him for years. When I moved to New York in 2005, I took the train over to South Slope, where they lived together. I'd found their building and walked up the four flights of stairs, expecting to be warmed by the face of an old friend. Together again! But, Ana stood at the door cold and thin, too thin, and pale. Only her eyes gave heat, but not the warming kind. I didn't see Mauricio that day, but I saw his bruises on Ana's arms. Deep purple thumb prints on her bicep. I'd run my fingers across the ragged cuts that scarred her wrist. "I didn't do it to hurt myself," she said. "I did it to hurt him."

I tried to warn Ana, "That guy Jake es malo. I can see it in his eyes."

"No, girl," Ana said. "You're not seeing what I'm seeing."

Jake sent me an email to my work account asking for my "professional discretion in the matter." He promised they really were in love. That she needed his help. I couldn't imagine what she needed him for, so I didn't reply. I tried calling Ana a few more times, suggested hang outs, but she was always *too busy*. Even though I worried about her, I kept my distance. I wanted her to be Ana, to stand on her own two feet, not wrapped around somebody else's.

* * *

A few weeks after running into Jake, I saw another ex-client out in the world. Michael. After working at Martina's, I sometimes went for dinner at an Italian restaurant in the Theater District. A place I couldn't actually afford, but justified as "self-care." I looked up from my food to see him with a woman his age and two teenage kids, sitting right across the restaurant from me. I'd seen Michael every week for two years before he disappeared. He'd told me he was single. He'd said something about moving to Westchester to be near his dying mother. I can't remember. What I did remember, while watching him delicately slice his steak, was the hotel on Lexington. A cold light beamed through a floor to ceiling window. I laid my hand on his warm chest and watched his breath quicken and tears stream out of his eyes. "I didn't know I could feel this way again," he said.

"I'm so glad you can feel," I replied and let my eyes beam with joy. Not for his emotions, but 'cause I knew each tear would turn to money in my hand. Michael and his family all looked unhappy, like no one could bother to think of anything to say. The woman, especially. She stared at the single noodle skewered on her fork, apparently lacking all appetite.

The teenage girl knocked over her water glass, and the woman chucked a napkin at her. Michael looked up with a face full of desperation. He saw me: The secret. He met my eyes, but looked right through.

It scared me. The secrecy of the secret. I felt my body slide out of focus. Could anyone actually see me? Was I disappearing from the knowable earth? I decided then, the next time Ana came around I'd tell her everything. But almost a year went by until she called, and a lot happened that year.

I had two shows, and started with a new instructor who would say things like *taxidermy is a still life that used to have a heartbeat.* I'd look at the piles of fur and tooth and glass eyes. I'd think about Ana, our after school adventures, that moment she turned into the sun, squinted her eyes and sent me a purple lipstick air kiss through the wind. I'd imagine Ma, still a girl, in the bed of a pick up truck tracing the constellations with her eyes. She rode North—to the very country funding the violence she'd escaped from—carrying with her a civil war in her own body; the sleeping cancer cells awoke and grew wild.

I called Ma, who I'd barely spoken to since leaving California five years earlier. When I left, she had remission status, three triumphant daughters, one tit, a mountain of medical bills, and a lab technician's cell phone number. That number was the only thing on her mind.

She didn't sound happy to hear from me. "Vos sabes que your sisters are driving me crazy," she said and made a sound like a whimper. "You're the only one of all the girls who can make it on her own."

"You ok?"

"Come back. Aqui te esperamos."

"Mamá, no. I'm moving to the desert."

"Don't let your ideas get in the way of our life. Besides, how will you make money in a desert?"

My younger sister called me later that week to tell me the cancer had returned. She asked if I could send more money. So, I started seeing guys I'd never usually see. One of them, a doctor, wrote me a prescription for tiny, oval-shaped pills that rolled all the secrets right off my skin, like water off of waxed hide. Every centavo went to Ma.

* * *

When Ana finally called it was a freak snow storm in spring. She told me she was getting married, and her voice sparkled like she'd done something bad and gotten away with it. I invited her over to drink her excitement away. Through the glass window of the building's door, I saw her waiting on the snowy stoop, looking like a lady who buys her clothes at department stores instead of thrift shops. Her tangled chocolate hair covered in flurry, bare hands flaunting a glistening diamond ring. She should've worn gloves on such a cold day. Even though it was the middle of April.

"Raquel!" Ana said throwing her arms over my shoulders. The icy flakes on her wool scarf melted against my cheek. "Where have you been?"

As happy as I was to see her again, something inside me, a small but well-armored door, slammed shut. I shuffled in slippers back towards my apartment. "Right here," I said. "But you have the exciting news."

Ana threw her coat over the arm chair by the radiator and held out her hand. "My Christmas present," she said. But all I could see were the shiny scars cross-hatched along her inner arm.

"Christmas present?" I said. "So you got engaged months ago. Everything must be going well." I headed to the refrigerator. "Want a beer? Or, I can mix a vodka something."

Ana pulled two bottles of sparkling wine from her purse. "This is a celebration, right?" She yanked out a cork, which shot off and smacked the ceiling. We sat around the wood table in the kitchen, next to the open window. I hadn't seen my wild thing for a few days. Her kibble sat untouched. I called out to her, worried that she'd froze to death. Wild thing! The only sound outside was the pat, pat of snow falling on more snow. Ana poured the pretty liquid into mugs. The bubbles puffed in applause.

I asked her about wedding plans.

"All we know for sure is that we're going to Cancún for our honeymoon," she said.

"Oh," I replied. "How's Jake's Spanish?"

Ana reached over to the open window and yanked it closed. "It's too cold in here."

"So how did this happen? Why Jake? I mean he's so—"

"Girl, I'm in love." Ana's eyes seemed suddenly vulnerable. "Can you believe it?"

I put down my mug of wine, ready to tell her everything. But my stomach knotted and my hands tingled with nerves. I reached into my purse, fingered around for an oval pill, found one, and swallowed it with my spit. As soon as it touched my tongue, I started to relax. "I have something you should try on." From my closet, I pulled out a black garment bag, and hooked it over the bathroom door. The dress is cut like a calla lily, simple, an immaculate white, embroidered with swanlike patterns.

"Que fancy," Ana said. "Where'd it come from?"

"Michael bought if for me."

I handed it to her; the weight felt satisfyingly heavy like a thick chain. She took the dress and it caught the sunlight from the window and glowed like something holy. Or maybe that was just the pill working.

"Who's Michael?"

I took another sip of wine and Ana wrestled off her tight blue jeans, flashing me a ludicrous pair of floral print undies. I scanned the back of her body for purple and blue signs of Jake's hands. I saw nothing. Michael had taken me shopping for an outfit to wear to dinner. I'd tried on that white dress and fell in love. All the sales guys asked if Michael and I were getting married, and he blushed like a bolo. I chose a pair of black stilettos to wear with it, but had to sell them when I came up short on rent one month. To me, they'd matched perfectly: The matte black and violent heel punctured the heart of the innocent dress.

Ana pulled the thin straps over her shoulders. I zipped her up, and the fabric sucked tight against her curves. She twisted her hair on top of her head, held it with one hand, the other posed on her hip. "Would you marry this?"

"Hell no," I smiled.

Ana stuck her tongue out, then made her face real serious. She walked barefoot across the hardwood floors toward the full-length mirror, like an enchanted girl in a story book. Like a bride. The mirror stands beside my desk, and I followed Ana there. The room smells musty in that corner, an inside smell. The sculpture I was working on then was a flying raccoon. Balanced on her hind legs, human-like paws groping in front of her as though sleep walking. I'd run a thick metal wire through the scavenger's back where eventually the wings would go. I made the wings myself from the feathers of four different birds: rusty brown turkey feathers, speckled quail, zebra- striped ewing, and dagger-red pheasant plumes.

Ana walked back to the table and popped the other bottle, white smoke curled around her hand.

"Ana," I said. "There's something I need to tell you." I imagined my body as it had been, half a life time ago. The tightly compressed knots of passion that sprang out like cactus flowers in spring. That day, it was spring and still snowing. "I'm a sex worker." I thought saying sex worker would make it sound like a white collar job.

She put on a disbelieving smile. "You're selling pupusa? Are you for real?"

I explained that I'd never be able to make my art and send money home if I wasn't sellin' pupusa. How actually, it's a great job with the exception of a few shitty guys.

"But at least I'm getting paid to deal with them," I said.

The air in the room suddenly went still. I told her the dress she had on was a gift from a client, she touched the fabric on her hips. "But it's so classy."

She tugged the zipper down and turned her back to me. But, I saw. On the thickest part of her thick brown thighs, scars piled in a lumpy keloid mess. Line upon line, some as wide as a finger, some as thin as a scalpel blade.

"Don't tell me Jake did that."

"I did." she said casually as she hung the dress back in the garment bag. "We all have our secrets."

I've seen her undressed a hundred times before, but right then her body felt like an extension of my own that had been amputated. A ghost limb. I reached out my hand to touch the scars. They were smooth. Topographical. An overgrown thicket of feeling. My skin tore from voice box to vulva, my insides crawled slowly onto my lap. I grabbed my bag and dug around for another white pill. I never took two. Especially after drinking.

"You started dating Jake too soon after Mauricio. I knew it was a bad idea."

She'd put her clothes back on, and sat in the arm chair tying her boots. She shook her head, and said nothing.

"Why Jake, Ana? I *know* guys like that."

I tried to stand but the room blurred. I steadied myself against the window, then flung it open. Fresh snow fluttered in.

"What's wrong with you?" Ana asked. "Where are you?"

"I know Jake," I said, settling myself back in the chair like the mess I was.

"You think you're funny, but actually you're fucked up. For real."

"It's true." I said, "Ask him."

"I'm out." I heard Ana's voice float around me, but she'd disappeared. Or maybe I had. It's ok. Everywhere, everyday, people, relationships, memories, they disappear. Maybe someday they emerge out of nothing, like they'd been there all along. Like they'd been sleeping and now they're awake. Like they were just waiting to be found. That night, I reappeared on the floor next to the kitchen table. Wild thing lay on my chest, her sharp claws grasping and contracting into my skin. She put her muzzle up to mine, yellow fangs bared, her soft breath tickled my nose.

"You ok?" I asked her. "I thought I'd lost you."

In July, Ma sent me a picture from the wedding. She'd been taking her mandatory walk on South Van Ness and seen the procession coming out of a church. Ana wore a shimmering ankle length dress with a beaded shawl across her shoulders. Her smiling idiot husband held her left arm and her stone-faced mother the right. Ma wrote, *You should have been there, hija. Dónde estás?* My cheek stung like I'd been slapped, again.

Months later, I ran into Ana on the street. We stopped and stared like we'd seen ghosts, before grabbing each other into a breathless hug. I told her about the picture. That she had looked happy on her wedding day.

She shrugged and told me the news. Her mother had been contacted by her cuñada. Ana's father's remains were identified in an unmarked grave with the bodies of other resistance fighters. Her mother was traveling back to El Salvador for the first time since she left thirty years before.

"No shit," I said. "Aren't you going with her?"

"I can't get away," Ana replied. Then she asked me if I still planned to run away to the desert.

"Some day."

"Tell me when." She squeezed my arm. "I'll meet you there."

But the July night Ma sent me their wedding picture, I wasn't sure if I'd ever see Ana again. I tried the dress on. It glided over me with a sensual slickness, but the rigidity of the embroidery was armor-thick. I walked around the apartment on my tippy toes pretending to be a bride 'til I got bored. Early in May, I'd flushed all the pills down the toilet and tried sobriety on for size. It fit for a while. I drank two cups of black coffee, took the dress off and kicked it across the wood floor. Naked, in front of the mirror, I wondered at the outside of my body: brown eyes, black hairs, purple labia, amber skin. I saw beneath the skin too: The bald red muscles and the network of veins and organs. Everything, really, is beneath the skin.

I took the scalpel from my desk and sat at the kitchen table, set the cold, thin blade just below my elbow and pressed down. I felt the skin split before the electric shock of pain shot up my arm and around my skull. My head filled with a sound like metallic waves; my fingers pulled the blade towards my wrist for the length of an exhale. Blood slowly rose to the surface. I peered inside, wishing I could see all the pieces of Ana that are stitched into me. My wild thing purred at the window. She looked in with her huge eyes and walked delicately onto the table, tail swishing side to side. She sat long enough to know my secret, then turned around, hopped off the window ledge and into the night.

Originally published in our Winter 2020-2021 Issue, *The Fiction Issue*
Featured in *Best Microfiction 2021*

Unfading

Nathalie Handal

Find me in the room midway between life and death, she said. Her hair wrapped in a rope of clouds tied to the sky. Her neck bent by a man's hand, her tongue suspended, one eye hidden, and an old man trying to mine her mind. Men tried to write her for a century, and other eternities. Their head spun in place. Their rage so loud she stopped hearing it. Telephone wires ran through her body and tugged her in different directions the way exile does. The way the world falls and the sea begs when love limps. The way numbers climb the wind like death tolls when oppressors are free.

The dead always come alive if they didn't die right. An Andean Condor came and stared. The walls sweating blood. Suddenly they appeared: Sor Juana Inés de la Cruz, Manuelita Sáenz, Juana Azurduy de Padilla, La Pola, Paixão Pagu, Tania LaGuerrillera, las hermanas Mirabal, las Madres de la Plaza de Mayo, las Abuelas de la Plaza de Mayo—speaking the myths, loading theirwords, and singing songs she hadn't discovered yet. They said: *No one will tell you where the water begins in your body nor where the blue getsbluer. It's a question of power. Explore the ruins. Draw the maps of deaths and damages and desires. Dive into her deep. Deep into hererotic. Discover the way back to her dream, your dream, and we will never disappear.*

Appeared in our Spring 2016 issue, *Atravesando*

Love Story for a Foreign Girl

Fiona Cheong

1.

Tell yourself, at least he's kind. You don't know this for sure, but the odds are good—look at all his gifts. Roses yesterday (not cheap), Hershey's Kisses today (too obvious). You'll realize this one day far in the future, but for now, you're nineteen and only six months out of your father's house—what do you care? Tell yourself that Americans don't beat their wives—you know this because you've seen it on TV—in America, husbands buy their wives diamond rings, cruise ship tickets, Maytag washing machines, and say "I love you" on the phone. In America, husbands and wives kiss in public, call each other "Baby," go away on second honeymoons. Actually, you have witnessed none of it yourself, but any day now, you believe you will.

This one, he's not quite what you were expecting, but he's all right, weight and height notwithstanding. Tell yourself he's not fat, he's stocky—just a little on the heavy side. He's also not tall, not even by Singaporean standards—the first time he came up to you in the cafeteria line, you were looking him straight in the eye, which means he's not even as tall as your tallest cousin, who with your other cousins have remained on the other side of the Pacific—but then, what do you need a tall one for? Looks aren't supposed to matter and you're not superficial. Remind yourself you're not superficial, having been raised among temples and oranges offered on red kitchen altars to the Buddha of Great Compassion. Remind yourself, at Thaipusam, your neighbors walked unscathed on hot coals during the festivities, their skeletal shoulders bare beneath the equatorial sun. That's the world you're from, not this America of plump skin and overwhelming dinner portions and expensive bits of clothing protecting almost nothing. Remind yourself whose daughter you are, whose granddaughter, whose niece, whose pupil.

"You have such a spiritual face," he tells you, his middle finger on a slow expedition up the inside of your thigh. No other guy has ever tried to get this far with you and when he flicks back the hem of your panties and slips in at the crotch, you're wetter than you thought you'd be. His finger wiggles around the mouth of your vagina, warm and thick as a cocktail sausage. You're not sure if you want to go on—you think, maybe not, because suddenly he's leaning close and his breath on your face makes you claustrophobic. Say nothing. Think about the time your cousins lowered you in the wooden bucket, farther and farther down the old church well. "Sekali jatoh, then how?" your aunts scolded the eldest, Gabriel, who was thirteen at the time, when they found out. You had thought it, too, in the well—you had thought that you might fall, the cold air plastered to your neck like mold. You survived that. You can survive this.

(No one's told you, yet, that sex doesn't have to be survived so meanwhile) tell yourself he's kind, not stingy with his money where you're concerned. Besides, he's gentle with his fingers, and since no guy's ever gotten this far with you, feel free to mistake surprises for pleasure. Let him slide one finger in, then two. Forgive the accidental scrape of nail, the searing heat of sudden blood. Someday, everything about him will become ordinary. This figment of knowledge presses on your chest, clogs your throat like dust—voices from another room thicken in your ears, threading you back to your father's house. So look up, while you can, at Orion's Belt spreading so gloriously behind the maple leaves. At the first clink of buckle, bite your lower lip. Breathe slowly when he unzips. Turn your cheek to the ground and smell this American grass against your hair.

There are women everywhere who are alone—spinsters like your Koko Mathilda even though she's gorgeous, widows like some of your other aunts who will never re-marry.

Tell yourself you're lucky.

Later, when washing your panties in the dormitory sink, gaze in the mirror. Find his words in your mother's expression that everyone who's known you since you were a child says you carry in your eyes. *You have such a spiritual face.* Against the bated fluorescent breath of this fall night on a university campus at the edge of your new world, follow the rise of your family's cheekbones, the compressed triangle of your father's nose, the mild downturn of his lips. No one has ever called you pretty, though an uncle did comment, once, on your pleasant smile. Pretty was reserved for your cousins Maureen, Noreen and Doreen, Gabriel's sisters who helped lower you down the well. You are no fool. You're aware that *pleasant* isn't the same as *pretty*, and neither is *spiritual.* But *spiritual* has brought you flowers and chocolates and who knows what else is waiting up ahead? Spiritual brought you an actual date, with a movie and popcorn thrown in, and someone wanting to make love to you under the stars. So *spiritual* is all right. More than all right.

Pay attention now. You don't know it, yet, but here's your formative moment. You're not superficial. You're spiritual, because as you will soon learn, your past is *the East*, full of the rustle of beaded screens swinging between what's real and not real. Your past is Susie Wong, Marco Polo, a twilight without geography. Pay attention. This is the mystery that you are on the brink of becoming in America. It's your ticket into the American heart.

2.

Now the going gets tricky. You've got to get serious about your accent, that ocean lilt from the other room, English pronounced as if it weren't English, your family's British Commonwealth grammar all mixed up. Your Koko Stella complaining about your youngest uncle and his girlfriend, about their exhibitionist behavior, how they're always hugging and fawning over each other. "T'ak seronoh, those two. Every time they go jalan, must pulok-pulok. Sudah kena spotted-lah, last night. And by whom, you know? By Madam Big Mouth herself. You see-lah, boleh mati, t'ak?" Koko Stella, your father's married sister, your mother's kindergarten friend and Gabriel's mother, bustles around inside your head, her voice pumping you full of memory. She wears batik colors and a hair net, smokes cigars with your uncles and has almost nothing good to say about the younger generation, except when it comes to you. You she loved, too obviously and too much. Don't forget that old church well, the receding circle of afternoon sky, your cousins' faces peering down in shadow. Tell yourself it's okay to let go. Start with Koko Stella. When putting her in a story for Creative Writing 202, catch every "lah" in mid-flow. Leaping as it did from another language, anyway, the word is merely pace—untranslatable. Slice it off. Koko Stella would want you to let go. Wouldn't she? She would want you to build a life, make the most of your time in America, be happy. You suspect she'd feel differently if she knew you wouldn't be going back, so don't tell anyone you won't be going back. Don't tell anyone you've already got yourself a boyfriend, who's stocky, not fat, and says "I love you" on the phone, and calls you "Baby" in bed. They won't guess if you don't tell. You're twenty and barely two years out of your father's house. You haven't even lost your accent, though you've learned to dangle "cool" and "dude" and "whassup" off your sentences like Navajo silver, as if you were some Asian chick from California.

You've learned to high five.

While no one's looking, read *The Woman Warrior*, *House on Mango Street*, and *Notes of a Native Son*. Read *The Way to Rainy Mountain*. In coffee houses, on the bus, in the aisles at K-Mart, count to yourself the number of Americans with bones like the bones of faces that help you sleep. Eventually, when you close your eyes, you will not miss the lullaby of frogs in the long grass, the billowing fragrance of orchids and frangipani and the gamelan call of the bamboo. You will forget that incense no longer wafts up the stairs, floating prayers for prosperity and health past your door.

Tell yourself it's all for the best. Remind yourself, you want the future more than memory.

Get used to the phrase, "people of color." Think of yourself as "we." When asked, "Where are you from?" if your boyfriend's not around, say, "San Francisco." Say, "Seattle." Say, "Queens, New York." Any one of these will do. When asked, "But where are your parents from?" say, "San Francisco." Say, "Seattle." Say, "Queens, New York."

Always answer the phone when it rings. When your boyfriend asks, "Don't you think it's time you told them?" tell him you will, soon. When he says, "Don't you want to get married?" don't panic. Remember that Europeans have been imagining the East for generations—you have an entire culture to use as an excuse. Say, "My father's very Chinese. He needs some time to get used to the idea of my marrying a non-Chinese." Don't tell him about your father's blondie girlfriend—how on your fourteenth birthday, your father came home drunk with a new German secretary from the office who giggled and blurted out her name, *Regina*, (a hard *g*), while your aunts were handing out slices of cake to your classmates and Sister Marie, who taught music and folk dancing during the week, and aikido on Saturdays, was putting Barry Manilow on the turntable. Your boyfriend will ask, "How much time?" and perhaps you'll feel a window springing open, an opportunity for escape. Don't take it. You don't know enough about the quality of the other fish in the sea, the ones available to you—keep in mind, no one has yet called you pretty.

Say, "Do you love me? Do you love me enough to wait?" It'll buy you a bit of time. Meanwhile, write *hard*, *card*, *marred*, *Harvard*, *tarpaulin*, on a blank page in your checkbook and carry this with you everywhere. Practice enunciating these words at least six times a day. Roll the r on the fleshy middle of your tongue, not too harshly—just a soft purr like the crawl of waves on a windless afternoon.

It's a delicate balance: You're spiritual, but you don't want to be F.O.B. You may be *Third World*, or *Oriental*, or just plain exotic, but you sure as hell don't want to be *Fresh Off the Boat*.

3.

So it happens sooner than you expect. That's all right. You've had your own fantasies for a while—you can't get wet without them anymore, which Louella Ruiz, who's from Austin, Texas, and is your best friend here, tells you is absolutely normal. What Louella means is: Of course, everything about a lover will become ordinary. "It's never like it was at the beginning, Anna," she says, her black hair blacker than yours in the wintry light, her voice like a bell in the chilled December air. Louella's not much older than you, but has been married since she was sixteen and lives in the apartment next-door with Miguel, who makes good money as a chef in the fancy French restaurant near the campus. Louella and Miguel were high school sweethearts and have a daughter, Sasha, who's five and wants to be an Olympic gymnast when she grows up. They call you "Anna"—it's the name you go by—only your boyfriend still calls you "Su Chin" (you realized too late, you never should have shown him your passport), and only in the letters from home, people still say, "Dear Gemok," or, if it's one of your cousins writing, especially Doreen (who's just gotten engaged and in a year will marry into one of the wealthiest families on the island), she'll use the English version, "Dear Fatso," which irritates you because it's not as if you haven't long shed your pubescent fat. By American standards, you're even skinny. Still, it's not Doreen's fault she doesn't know this. You haven't been home in three years and you've ignored the various ways people have found to ask, "Why?" You can't even send home photographs taken with your boyfriend's camera—the ones of you alone, clothed. Your father wouldn't notice a thing, but your aunts, especially Koko Stella, and Koko Mathilda, who seldom spoke but gazed out of windows with such attentiveness throughout your childhood—they've watched you since the hour you were born. Koko Stella held you while your mother bled beneath the dazzling hospital lights. (Your father, you've heard, wasn't even there.) Show your aunts a photograph of you now, and they might begin to guess. So it's all right. Forgive yourself, and them, for what you must do. Send home only your semester grades. Send home brief, poker-faced aerograms. Add a picture postcard now and then for variety. And always sign yourself, "Gemok." When you feel the urge to spill the truth, you've got Louella. She doesn't smell like any of your aunts, but her arms are warm and sincere, and conversations with her carry no complications.

"What you've got to decide is," says Louella, "are you still in love with him? If you are, then both of you have got to work this out, whatever it takes. Know what I mean?"

You know what she means. Conversations like the one you and Louella are having have taken place before, are taking place, all over the world, and nowadays even on TV. (You've seen the interviews. You understand, there will always be women who have it worse than you.) When you found the earring in your boyfriend's pocket last week, there was nothing unique about that—a single earring, good-luck jade, a sheen of green not commonly available in American Chinatowns. You never wear jade. (Too F.O.B.) Nothing unique about your racing heart when you put it back, dropping the earring slowly in his pocket like something fragile, possibly precious, irreplaceable. When you counted the condom packets in his dresser drawer, there was nothing unique about the fact that too many were missing. And in the mirror, your face was a face you've seen before, long ago in your father's house.

What puzzles you is the hurt. Why should any of it still hurt? It's not as if your own mind hasn't wandered during sex over the last few months.

"Of course it hurts," says Louella. "Some bitch has got her fingers in your pie, Girlfriend. That always matters. So my question to you is, do you still love your man?"

The question is huge.

These last few months, you've lingered in the bathroom longer after sex, taking longer to wash off. There's a Cuban with eyelashes to die for who saunters past you every Tuesday afternoon in Shakespeare 330, on his way to the back row. All faded dungarees and muscle, biceps blossoming in white T-shirt cut-off sleeves, a smile so sweet, you're blushing every time you catch his eye. You've told Louella his name. Joaquin. You're friends with his best friend Mikey. They're all from Newark, New Jersey—Mikey, Joaquin, and the girlfriend Celia (who works at K-Mart and doesn't attend the university)—it's where they grew up after their families came over. You've seen Celia. She's gorgeous like Koko Mathilda, the kind of gorgeous that hushes a room and renders almost every kind of man speechless. It's beyond losing weight, beyond using the right make-up and having a good haircut and wearing the right colors. It can be dangerous, that kind of gorgeous, and now you think maybe for Koko Mathilda it was—something happened to her before you were born, the shape of which hovers like a ghost no one will mention in your father's house. You've told Louella you don't mind that you can never be that gorgeous. You know in real life, a fish like Joaquin will always swim way beyond your reach. You've told her he helps you out, anyway (wink, wink)—in the bathroom after sex.

Only lately, even that hasn't worked.

Say, "I don't know," this time, even if it makes your voice faint, so faint, Louella's leaning toward you over the ginger cookies and the banana bread, her dark eyes frowning. She's good at feeling people out, so she knows something's up. What she doesn't know is that you don't know exactly what's up. You would tell her if you could, because you want to tell somebody. You want somebody to know that the ground's no longer firm beneath your feet—it's been gathering water, sea grasses, whirlpools.

And it's been happening for a while, before last week, which is why last week shouldn't matter. And yet, it does. So say again, "I don't know," because that's as close to the truth as you can bear to be for now.

Breathe in. Count one, two, three. Breathe out. Smile and withdraw. Pretend you're on *Donohue* or *Oprah*. Add: "He's been good to me, except for this. You know how he is. He's a kind person. We're just under a lot of stress. You know we're applying to grad schools. I mean, his top choice is Harvard Law, and there are good writing programs in Boston but what if I could get into Iowa? Or Stanford? Or Cornell? Having to choose is just so stressful."

"So what does that mean? You're going to try and work it out?" asks Louella, her tone lumpy as fudge because she'd rather just cut to the chase.

You don't want to lose her friendship by lying, so don't. Shrug your shoulders but not blithely. Say again, "I don't know." Cut yourself a chunk of banana bread, wielding the knife carefully because it's after five o'clock. The sun's gone down, but neither of you has moved to turn on the light. Breathe slowly, evenly, the way Sister Marie once taught you. Breathe as if your heart's still whole.

4.

Wait until daylight, after you've had some sleep, and your boyfriend's out of the apartment again. You'll want your wits about you so the break is clean. You'll want to pack only what you need, but also everything you'll need, so you won't have to come back and risk dragging matters out. If you came back, you might change your mind, end up staying, end up trying to work things out.

It's not as if anyone has yet called you *pretty*, but lately, fewer and fewer Americans have been asking you where you're from. You're almost four years out of your father's house. You've learned how to fade your dungarees just right, and to call them "blue jeans" in public. You wear Timberlands in the snow and a Yankees baseball cap in summer. You no longer hunch your shoulders when you're in a bikini. You shave your legs. You sunbathe.

Most important of all: a famous and respected writer who on Friday visited the fiction workshop you're in told you later, at a reception being held in his honor, that he found your story (a half-true, half-made-up story about Koko Mathilda) fascinating. He called it "deeply engaging." He called you "highly gifted." He gave you his phone number in New York City and said, "If you happen to be in the city, call. We'll have dinner."

Do not accept his invitation (you've heard the rumors about him) but ponder its significance. You're not yet *pretty*, but your options are expanding.

So when your boyfriend's footsteps no longer echo in the stairwell, pack the essentials first: your wallet, checkbook, passport, ATM card, university I.D. Wrap your jewelry in a washcloth, what you wore from home (the ruby earrings Koko Stella told you were your mother's and the gold bangle that was your grandmother's) and even what your boyfriend gave you, because none of it was cheap. Retrieve the photographs. Count them—make sure you have all twelve. These go straight into your backpack, along with your toothbrush, two Stayfree napkins just in case, a notebook, two pens. Also pack toothpaste, shampoo, soap—one of each will do because you won't be traveling far, only to a room you've noticed advertised for rent above the Laundromat across town, on the street where Miguel's a chef in that fancy French restaurant, which is far enough.

Pack two pairs of dungarees, all your panties, four clean T-shirts and this semester's course books in your duffle bag. Leave the rest. Write a letter so your boyfriend will feel free to sell what he can and donate what remains to Goodwill.

When you leave your key on the kitchen table and shut the front door so it locks behind you, remind yourself this is all for the best.

(One day you'll know that it truly is so until then) do what others like you do, what women before you have done, what your daughter, too, may have to do—fake it. Fake it until you don't have to anymore.

Originally published in our Summer 2019 issue, *Inheritance*

The One-Eyed Bat!

Yalitza Ferreras

The guy I'm dating in Ann Arbor is The One-Eyed Bat! He wrestles with a mask over one eye. He's from a Mayflower family in Massachusetts, and he goes to Mexico to wrestle Lucha Libre-style. He jumps from the ropes onto his opponents and ensnares them with his black velvet bat wings. It's an art thing.

When he drives us to Detroit, to photograph urban ruins, we pass this wiener sign outside the factory where they make them on Holbrook Street. The wiener is in big red neon, disproportionate in size to the building it is attached to by a giant skewer. The first time I saw the sign, I gasped and screamed out, A big red wiener! and he just nodded as the wiener cast its shadow on us, didn't even crack a smile. The wiener sign says "Kowalski" and is in the city of Hamtramck, just outside of Detroit. Has there ever been a more delightful name for a city? H-A-M-T-R-A-M-C-K. It needs more vowels. I think about the missing vowels, and phonemes and epenthesis, and I think that Hamtramck seems like enough when you say the name, but not when you see the word. Sometimes he takes my left hand in his and blows warmth into it as we drive on ice-covered streets, and I feel happy. The first time he took me to Ypsilanti for another art thing, and we approached the city's old water tower, named the Word's Most Phallic Building by entities that declare such things, I didn't say anything as we drove by its girthy base on Summit Street, the highest point in the city. He was talking about the themes of masculinity in his Lucha Libre project. Summit Street! I was hoping he would notice the delight on my face, but he didn't. Okay, so I try to engage with his work, I say, uropatagium instead of fixating on penis. We talk about studies on how bats use their uropatagia in flight thrust, but when I call the membrane their bat butts, I lose him. So anyway, what scientists are saying is that wings are obvious, but bat butts are important, too.

And then we get to Detroit, and he makes art. I wander around the decay of these abandoned buildings, and I politely ease out of his frame, spinning on split floorboards, risking my life on tippy toes. He takes these photographs that make the desolation look like a movie set built just for him to explore themes of loss of industry and people. After elegiac pronouncements, he lights the shot, makes use of something that was once useful. Then, we fuck.

I am supposed to be writing. He's a multi-medium artist. I don't mean multi-media. He sings and plays guitar and dances and takes pictures, and he mentioned something about a unicycle once, and he makes films, and this wrestling thing too. He must've exhausted his parents. My mother says that I was sometimes so quiet she had to poke me to make sure I was okay.

I walk around. I don't understand why everyone is in love with these ruins. I prefer the parts of Detroit with people in them. All of these places look like my childhood memories of burned out squats in Bushwick, where I was born brown like everyone around me, you know, before Bushwick was cool. Detroit feels familiar, but this is not my city, these are not my ruins. He is photographing a heap of books with mushrooms growing out of them. These dead books are my worst nightmare. I am standing off to the side under an art-deco archway, its red, blue and orange tiles fallen off and strewn at my feet. A faint light glows through a hole in the floor. I take a step forward, and a loud clanging echoes through the space. He looks up and tells me to be careful, and I think about pressing down harder. I want to make an offering to this place. I picture my congealed guts dangling off the jagged entrails of the building. I slide down carefully instead. I put down a knee. Other knee. Head tilts. I slowly uncoil my scarf from around my neck. I call him over.

Afterwards, we go to the gallery in Detroit where he's showing the photographs of himself soaring above Mexicans in his flappy wings, black shorts and Lucha Libre mask. In one image, he stands on the ropes of a makeshift boxing ring outdoors in a field or what looks like someone's backyard. He is gritting his teeth, stomach muscles bulging. He is beautiful. His tousled white-blond hair is peeking out of the half-face head mask that makes him The One-Eyed Bat! His body looks like a classical statue looming over his opponents.

They say that bats see better than humans. What I see is the torso from a David about to topple on all these smaller, rounder, browner men, but I don't say it. I start waving my hands around the space. I tell him what I think about the lighting, how to arrange the photographs, not what I think about white bodies coming down on brown bodies in their own backyards.The gallery owner comes over and smiles at me like, you guys are such a great couple. I just keep trying to make some arrangement out of the pieces and pointing at the walls.

10th Anniversary Issue

Author Comments

Yalitza Ferreras on "The One-Eyed Bat!"

What inspired this piece?

While I was pursuing a Creative Writing MFA degree at the University of Michigan, occasional forays into Detroit were a respite from the stresses of graduate school and the neat collegiality of my daily life in Ann Arbor. It seemed that Detroit "ruin porn" was featured everywhere, pictures of its urban decay the subject of countless photo essays along with articles explaining the city's decline. But Detroit felt like home, like Brooklyn when I was a kid, when the masses hadn't moved there yet. In the story, I wanted to capture that time, trips that felt like perverse glimpses of pre-gentrification.

Originally published in July 2017 online at asterixjournal.com

"The Past is Not Always Past:" A Conversation with Edwidge Danticat

Jessica Lanay Moore

Edwidge Danticat is an award-winning novelist and short story writer, known for her work on national identity, mother-daughter relationships, and diasporic politics. Born to Haitian parents, Danticat was raised by an aunt and uncle in Haiti until she was 12 years old, when she immigrated to New York to join her parents. After a childhood steeped in storytelling and literature, she published her first novel, *Breath, Eyes, Memory* in her early twenties to critical acclaim. Since then, outlets like *Harper's Bazaar* and *The New York Times Magazine* have routinely identified her as a rising star of contemporary influential writers. She has published over a dozen novels, as well as written several short stories and films.

Danticat spoke with Jessica Lanay Moore for *Aster(ix)* and *Sampsonia Way Magazine* about her literary influences, the relevance of the recent past, the role of race and performative whiteness, and acts of political and cultural engagement in an increasingly globalized world.

Jessica Lanay Moore: So my first question is probably the first question that everyone asks you, who are your writing influences or what writers have inspired you time and time again? Poets?

Edwidge Danticat: My greatest writing teachers were the oral storytellers in my family. The way my aunts and my grandmothers structured a story, the way they told a story, was very powerful for me as a little girl. And, the immediacy of an oral story, when you have an adult in front of you and they are gauging your response, and if you seem bored, or seem like you're falling asleep, they speed up the story. That's a very strong connection. So oral story telling was a powerful influence for me. And then when I started reading, the first book I received as a present when I was a kid was Ludwig Bemelmans' *Madeline*. Madeline's life was very different from mine. At the same time it wasn't, because she was living in a house filled with parentless children, or children whose parents you didn't know where they were, and that was very similar to the house I grew up in because my aunt and uncle looked after a lot of children of people in the family who had migrated to the US, Canada, and the Dominican Republic. So I grew up in a kind of kids' group home.

JLM: What is the relationship between joy, justice, brutality, beauty, and violence in your writing? There is a lot of verve around this idea that joy is a form of resistance in Black arts or Diaspora Black arts, and writing. You said that in your experience living in Haitian communities here in the United States, you've often found people being overly polite in the company of people who others know were instruments of brutality and violence, so what is your relationship with joy, in what seems like an unavoidable juxtaposition, in your work?

ED: I think joy is a kind of self-preservation against brutality and violence, and destruction in general. People who have had everything thrown at them with the goal of destroying them, still manage to find some kind of joy. That in itself is a miraculous victory; it is a triumph. I think that's why people often talk about resilience, which has become a sort of cliché. Sometimes I resist that whole label of oppressed people's resilience, but we do find ways to survive that are creative and that includes joy, and creativity itself, and certainly the arts, dance, song, painting, literature.

After the earthquake in Haiti, for example, people kept saying how Haitians are so resilient. And I would think that this resilience means that we can suffer more than other people, but there is something about finding joy in the middle of an environment that is meant to just destroy you, and I think that is what a lot of African Diaspora Arts emerge from … the blues, jazz, even the spirituals, or what they call Negro spirituals, that came out of slavery and merged into " I'll fly away" myth, stories, folktales, which are meant to be more than comfort, but are meant to take us outside of the present moment into some future we had to imagine.

There is an essay that I love by Alice Walker, "In Search of Our Mother's Gardens." I talk a little bit about it in [my 2011 book from Vintage] *Create Dangerously: The Immigrant Artist at Work*. In that essay, Walker talks about how women whose souls just yearn to be artists—in the sense that we now know artists–but because they couldn't in their time and place, they made their quilts. They planted their gardens. They did what they could, with this creativity that was being stifled inside of them. What do you do with the poetry in you if you are not allowed to read? You know, you sing it, you hum it. It comes out through the church. It comes out through these other means that are available to you. So, I just feel like joy as a means of survival is very important to counter all of the pain and cruelty we've been forced as a people to endure.

I think it's important to turn inwards now and then and find a bit of joy, in your family, in your work, within yourself, in order to survive everything that is going on in the world around you. Art is a big part of that, because you need some level of hope, or some level of joy—or at least satisfaction in the creation of art—in order to be able to create.

...Relations between Haiti and the Dominican keep reminding me how history is more than a shadow, and how cyclical it can be. Sometimes people look back at horrible things and think—Oh, this worked, let's try it again. And they may not murder people en masse, but find other ways to destroy them. They say that if we don't know our history, we are doomed to repeat it. It's just amazing to me how often, in different ways, we repeat our histories. The past is not always past. That to me is the lesson of writing [my 1998 novel] *The Farming of Bones.*

JLM: In the beginning of *Create Dangerously,* you quote Osip Mandelstam, "Only in Russia is poetry respected—it gets people killed," can you speak to this danger to create in the context particular to *Create Dangerously*, which is the immigrant writer's experience, and then on a wider scale as perhaps to what might be coming for writers who "other" period, whether they are immigrant or not in today's contemporary atmosphere.

ED: It is interesting to see this moment from the perspective of someone who grew up in a dictatorship. The dictatorship was already rolling along when I was born, so you just kind of land in the middle of it if you are born at that time. There are people in my family who saw the dictatorship emerge from the beginning. The dictatorship wasn't gradual. Back then, there was a coup and the guy takes the power and he is a strongman from day one. But I remember living through the Reagan era when I was a kid and hearing about immigration raids nearly every day. I remember living through the second George W. Bush era and seeing the post-September 11th 2001 wars begin, and seeing the Patriot

Act be put in place and seeing people debate in newspapers whether or not pouring water down someone's nose for an hour is torture. I feel like we are going back to a combination of those times where it was brute force and bombings, and accentuating otherness. I am also seeing a lot of artists engage more, even with simple acts. For example, if someone gets a prize and makes a speech, it is a different speech than it would have been four years ago. Artists are becoming more vocal. I think that's important. I think what will come out of this era is more engagement. That engagement is not always in the press but quietly in communities as well. We are seeing that engagement from our citizens as well as from our artists. That's really what I wanted to share when I wrote *Create Dangerously,* that these things have been happening around the world for a long time and that they keep happening. People can take over power who undo everything we know. That's not an anomaly. It's been happening forever. What's crucial is how people respond. I am hoping that life in the US these days will also make Americans more empathetic towards what other people have been going through around the world, and what other artists and citizens around the world have to sacrifice for their self-expression.

JLM: Your short stories and novels are very rich and specific. They call on the descriptive action that reads like Gabriel Garcia Marquez, while still having enough breath in the lines to offer some Voltaire-esque commentary from characters. And through these images you build community. Can you speak towards the religious and cultural braiding that happens in your work? And the relationship those have with politics?

ED: All of those things are weaved into daily life, into your need to go on living, or just go on about your day, which then involves what is going on in the country in general, what's going on in the world, in your personal relationships, your memory, your past, your spirituality. I think that all of that is embodied in the human being, and that's why I try to encompass all that when I write about a person. When I am writing about a person, I am writing about a community. And this involves writing about the different spiritual faiths and beliefs of those people and how that flows with or against the community. [My 2013 novel] *Claire of the Sea Light,* for example, is a book about a little girl, but she comes with a whole community. And not all of the stories I write show a whole community, but the community is always there. We are all part of these communities. We have these personal concerns, but we also have these global concerns, and those concerns are heightened when you are talking about people who have a lot of needs, who lack a lot of things, who have very urgent daily needs. I think it's also important to be also allowed existential crises. Our people, our characters too, should be able to ask who am I? Do I belong here? At the same time, they are looking for food. They are going to church and praying to get a visa to leave the country. They dance at weddings. Every character comes with a world and is a world to me. Every character embodies a history, a culture, different types of spirituality. So all of that comes in each of the stories that I write.

-

Editors' note: this interview has been condensed and edited for clarity. The entire original conversation is available to read online.

Originally published in our Winter 2020-2021 Issue, *The Fiction Issue*

Last-Last Resignation

Mubanga Kalimamukwento

1st March 2017

Lusaka.

Re: Resignation – Prisca Banda

Madam, many months now, you been talking at me, saying, 'Prisca, you need English if you want to be somebody.' You say this last word slow, pounding it into three small pieces that come out with your mouth squeezed like this and your nose pointing up. I take your meaning to be: *If I want to be some-bo-dy, like you, who can make your maid and garden boy scatter to look busy at the sound of your revving Subaru engine, I must add more English to my talking.*

So, with my Christmas bonus last year, I register myself into night school at Lusaka Girls' and start putting somebody-making English into my head.

And thank God, because now I can say my resignation without the trouble of looking in your eyes, which, when they are angry, can chase all the words from my mouth and push them back inside my throat.

This word, *resignation*, I pick it out of *Longman Dictionary of Contemporary English* in class last week. It mean *'an occasion when you officially announce that you have decided to leave your job,*' and '*when someone calmly accepts a situation that cannot be changed, even though it is bad.*'

Last time I am stop this job, it wasn't my own wanting, no. Yourself, you chase me. You call me 'dirty little thief!' of your nice, shining Brazilian wig—the one which you buy on nkongole from Bana Musebo. Even though, when Bana Musebo, she come to pinda you for her monies, I tell her that you fly to Dubai just that morning. In true, you have just run into the pantry, like one of those fat rats which hide behind the sack of mealie meal.

When you finally unlock the door and come out peep-walking, slow-slow, back into the kitchen, with your dress stinking of dry tilapia and your face no more the nice brown of groundnuts but the white of mealie meal, I keep my laugh buried on my inside. I just tell you, 'She's gone, Madam,' and keep on scrubbing the black burnings in a pot at the sink.

You say to me, 'Oh my gosh, Prisca, you're such a lifesaver!'

But one small month afterwards, Madam, you forget all the lifesaving I did by lying on you to Bana Musebo, and dress me in that dirty name: thief.

Thief, it mean to '*steal another person's property.*' Which, if I say the true, I do it sometimes, but only to the cooking oil because my own, it finish too-too fast. Plus, I know if I aks you, you'll just talk me: 'Prisca, you need to manage your salary better!' As if 500 kwacha, it is very big monies which need even to be manage. But your wigs? Never! Me, I like my hair in simple mukule just like this. Yet, even after I explain this, Madam, even after I beat my chest and swear, '*Akalumba fye*, Madam, it was not me,' you still chase me.

'Get out of my yard, you little thief! Don't dare bother me about your salary.' This was you shouting big, squeezing all your face into one tight ball like you ate too much impwa.

Quiet, I pack up my shame and fold it under my arm together with the yellow Shoprite plastic bag where I keep my spare clothes. I carry it out and walk back to Ng'ombe.

Two days go like this, with me having no job. But to tell you the true, it was no different than before, except I spend both of the days at Blessings Maid Centre instead of polishing your floors, and making your daughter, Lubuto, laugh when ZESCO takes away the electric and she can no more laugh at Disney Junior. I wait there for another Madam to walk in and say, like you, 'You, in the corner. You seem like a hard worker. Come with me!' I wait because I know that I still have enough beans at home to carry my stomach to the month-end. So, the only trouble that worry me then is where I should find the money to give my landlord his rent. But before this problem can press itself into the corner of my eyes and pound my head, my phone ring once.

'Hello, Madam,' I answer.

'Hello, Prisca,' you say, with your voice now butter soft. 'I have no one to take care of Lubuto. Could you please come?'

I know already that you have no one to watch Lubuto because that child takes many days to learn a person's face and longer even, to accept it. I know also that it isn't Lubuto making the butter melt and slide your tongue soft like this. You must have find your wig buried somewhere under the pile of clothes you haven't been able to fit for many months now because your stomach, after Lubuto, it stay swollen like you are too full. This is your *Sorry*.

Lubuto, she is just a baby—only one years, not even big enough for school, and it has only been two days. Too short for her to learn a new maid's face.

'Okay, Madam,' I say, 'I'm come.'

'You're such a darling, Prisca.'

Now, today, you forget the darlingness and put in its place, *pro-stute*. Madam, even for this paper, the word is too ugly. It's still paining me. My chest is still the heavy of cement brick from remembering how you say it so easy. 'I should have known you were just a *pro-stute*, Prisca!' With your eyes pointing at me straight as if you're talking me something simple like, 'Prisca, bring this to the car, please,' or maybe, 'Check on Lubuto, please, she's crying again.'

The worser thing is, you spit this ugly word in the front of Collins when already, you know, this garden boy has no respect for me. Each time you send me to tell him to water the flower bed, what does he do? He shout, 'Ah, *iwe*!' even flipping his hand like that, as if I'm his size. 'You're just a *kaboyi*, like me!' Like his big eyes are blind to see that: 1. I'm a maid who work inside the house and not outside with the dirty, and 2. I am two times his small sixteen-years age.

Worsest, you know me, I pray. You seen me with your own two eyes, wearing my blue-white Dorcus Mother uniform on the Sabbath mornings you bring Lubuto for me to take care of, even though I am off work. How can you now call me a *pro-stute* all because you find that big black pant swinging from the inside hinges of your bedroom door? Big black pant like that, which is not even to my size.

Madam, I beg you, listen me well here, please! That your husband—he was home, yes. For lunch only. I even serve him his favourite: curry chicken with fresh kalembula. I cook it exact the way he want, putting oil at the beginning and again at the end, in between sprinkling crushed chillies and garlic. While he eat, I make myself busy outside, polishing his shoes and reminding Collins to water the roses. Remember you find me on that same verandah? I was putting your husband's shoes to air out the 'five-day stink,' as you say.

Every Friday before this one, you never come home for lunch. Friday is when you get your eyebrows cut into the nice surprise-shape even if it not look like the TV womens. But this Friday, you drive in, rush out of the car and into the house before Collins or me can collect any packages or give you a word. You say, 'I forgot my purse, Prisca—just need to dash in and collect it quick—Lubuto give Mommy a kiss,' fast—fast like that, as if the words are chasing your feet.

Instead of purse, you find your bedroom door open like a mouth—inside it, your husband breathing like a man running, and that black pant stuck in the door like burnt meat between teeth.

It feel like the time start to crawl and then stop sudden when you rush back to slap me. If you are not busy calling me *pro-stute*, I could have tell you that Bana Musebo, she come today. If you are not too busy shouting, 'You little bitch! You bitch! You've been fucking my husband? Shit,' maybe I could have tell you how Bana Musebo, she did not even ask me, 'Is your Madam inside?' She walk into your house, proud on her pointy shoes like this, shaking her buttocks like two ripe mangoes begging to fall from the tree. Like that, she go straight into your bedroom with your husband following behind. Me, I keep myself outside because if I see nothing, I'll have no lies to tell. But even from out there, with the loud of tyres on Independence Avenue, and dogs barking at them through gates, your husband's voice comes running out, shouting, 'Fuck!' for all of Woodlands to hear it.

But, it like, the way your voice climb from alto to soprano quick, scare my own voice. Even when I open my mouth, nothing come out. In my head, I tell you how Bana Musebo, she's tiptoeing out of the kitchen door and through the back gate, holding her sharp shoes in her hands. If you just pause, small-small, between those bad words, I could've maybe point one small finger behind. You could turn your head and see; even the strap of her bra was looking out of her shirt to show you who *pro-stute is*, for true-true.

One last-last thing here, Madam: next Friday, maybe drive home early by small minutes. Twenty minutes, maybe. Enter the house soft. Maybe you catch Bana Musebo before she have a chance to put herself back together. *Coincidence*, say my dictionary: *'A remarkable concurrence of events or circumstances without apparent causal connection.'*

If it don't happen: good! But if it do, allow your tongue to move quick this time, like hot butter in a frying pan. Don't say, 'I need someone to watch Lubuto,' no. Say Sorry for true-true, this time.

Yours,
Prisca.

10th Anniversary Issue
Author Comments

Mubanga Kalimamukwento on "Last-Last Resignation"

How did this piece come about?

I wrote this story for a class I was taking during my MFA. The prompt was to write a resignation letter but use the skills we were learning in writing humour. I decided to channel the voice of my first and favourite nanny, who lived with my mom and me until I was six. At home, we mainly spoke Bemba, but she loved testing her English on me, especially when she wanted to pray. I was also thinking about when my kids were very little, learning how to talk and navigating three languages at once. Often, they jammed multiple languages into one sentence, but we understood them.

Appeared online in November 2017 at asterixjournal.com

The Girl With Two Brothers

Sejal Shah

When I was twelve or thirteen, we lived in the house on Old Massapoag Road, and I used to dream what I thought all girls dreamt: someone snatched me, began to work off my clothes. You were there watching. Your grey eyes troubled your face. You rescued me. You pushed him and his ski-mask aside. You yelled out various ways you would punish him. He ran through a side street, scaled a fence, disappeared. You stroked my face (how soft, you murmured). You kissed me. How marvelous, I thought. How miraculous! I'm breathing and I'm kissing at the same time. We ran, then walked past the high school, our blue sneakers breaking the dark. You saved the only thing worth saving. This is how our story always began.

My dreams stopped when I thought of wanting a camera—of needing some way to record. I wasn't thinking about shutter speed, about aperture, about flash.

My oldest brother was tired of my asking to borrow his things. Or of my borrowing them without asking. Before the idea of a camera, I thought of the usual things. Living in olden times, a secret conversation in a secret language (I was the only one who understood.) I thought of running away, of what I would save in my house in case of fire, which albums I would grab, and which dolls.

I was all about orphanhood, the plane from Chicago crashing—we would have to go live in California with my father's brothers—one of them was our legal guardian—and I wonder who thought to tell me that—is that what parents are supposed to tell, or did I ask them, knowing how these things go, knowing how these things may go. I was always asking: *Who will take care of me if you go? How will I live if you go?*

Did all children dream these things then, in quilts of birds and falls and forgotten red bicycles? I thought of how my parents would cry uncontrollably when I died at a young age from a devastating disease. I imagined the wake, their friends circling them, the plates of slightly stale cake, the enlarged photos of me wreathing the walls, the scrapbook with every Mother's Day and birthday card I had ever made, the slightly discolored green construction paper, school glue still shining in smudges. My older brothers would cry (I had almost never seen them cry), but they would have to force the tears—I was dead after all! For once, the applause I had been waiting my whole life for.

Or, if our parents died, perished in a plane crash, would we refuse to be shipped off to California? Would we live in an abandoned train car, next to the elementary school, in the bramble near where the middle school kids came to smoke and flick their red and yellow lighters? Would we flee to New Jersey, to our other uncle's house, refusing to leave the East Coast? Where would we play our secret game: the White Witch, the Purple Policeman, the Green Ghost, circling? My oldest brother had the banana-seat bike we both wanted. My middle brother had Matchbox cars he raced for hours. All I had was Lite-Brite and make-up head Barbie.

Perhaps our relatives wouldn't want all three of us—we would have to fight to be together—we would not let ourselves be split up. Or:

we'd have to fight to get to California, all three of us, crossing the Mississippi—like two cats and a dog, or two dogs and a cat. (In every scenario, I was a cat.)

I was a well-read child of all the usual fairy tales—I knew how it went. The parents never lasted beyond the first page. Some of the best ones had the parents dead before the book even began. Or the father was mean. Or the mother was crazy. Or the father was weak. Or the mother was dead. All you had was your brother, and in my case, I had two. All you ever had was your brother, and all the ways in which you hoped that he would—that any boy might—try to see you, recognize you, save you, because you were a girl, and you were worth saving. You were worth something.

* * *

We lived on Massapoag Road. I loved the sound: *Massapoag*. It meant great waters in a language no one I knew remembered. When I wasn't searching the ground for arrowheads or a perfectly smooth pebble, I had the regular battery of fantasies: death wishes for various family members. Imagining the grief, the unbearability of it all was one way to love them. So I wanted more than a regular camera (I was an unusual child, or perhaps very ordinary). I wanted an instrument to record people I had thought about or had seen. I wanted to be able to show others something that existed only in my head. I wanted to be able to remember. I was young enough not to realize that it is better to just let things go. A story is just another way to let things go.

This is one way to tell the story: You and me and the girl on Chestnut Street. Here is another: I wanted you to save me. You wanted me to save you. Did you understand that was what we were really saying? Why not choose me? The mental refrain of gym class, of sweat, of fourth grade come back to haunt.

Older brother #1 says: We'll kick his ass.

Older brother #2 says: *What* is that music you're listening to?

More books would have kept me out of trouble, but I welcomed her, trouble: running at night next to the horse farm, beer and fish tacos across the middle of the day, crouching by the guard rail, fiddle music on high; driving down 91, through Connecticut. We were on our way to New York, so there was no way to avoid Connecticut. I had always disliked Connecticut: connect and cut: telling you both things at once, not unlike a boy. When I was younger, maybe six or seven, I knew that states were male or female. Connecticut was clearly a boy. Vermont: a girl. New Hampshire is a boy: *Live Free or Die*. What girl do you know who would say that? We might say it, but we don't believe it. I don't believe it.

I always said more than a single girl should: dropping the names of old boyfriends, stupid words collecting in the corners of my mouth. These are all different ways to say: You are the absence that lingers.

Older brother #1 says: Remember my friend Pete, the mathematician? He's a nice guy.

You said you would soon know all my stories. As in a fairy tale, every week, I felt I had to give you a reason to leave, manufacture a reason for you to stay. You pointed out that you were turning into one of my stories. Even if this story is about you (and you knew there would be one) how do you know what I will squander to make the story better, and what I will keep, afraid?

I looked you up in the dictionary. I found you under save. There were many definitions and every one of them fit. Everything was about avoidance. The prevention of fatigue. As in: *to save one's longing.* This is what the dictionary said. *To anticipate one's desire and so to prevent. To save one's own hide or skin: To reserve or lay aside.* To keep from harm.

Older brother #1 says: I think you'd like him. He works for Intel. He knows how to ice skate.

This, then, is the frame; this, without a lens. I decided to take fewer classes. Shoving back folders, I instructed you in sun salutations in the living room, still in my work clothes—blouse, skirt, nylons. I watched you watch me, the candy-colored stripe of underwear when my shirt lifted away; we stripped in kitchen-blind sunlight after downward dog, after upward dog. We laughed through plank. Your mouth, disarming the buttons of my skirt. The sunlight, splitting us. Your nails, ruining my nylons. Track one on repeat, track nine on repeat, beer spilling onto the kitchen floor, beer spilling from your hand, your hand knocking everything over.

We walked to the pond they call lake and sat listening to the birds (loons? swans?). Something large from Canada. I wanted to believe they were a sign. Birds herald something in every book I ever read, and we all know how much books can help us in this world, can save us in this world.

Brother #1 calls me Chris, as in Evert Lloyd. Older brother #2 calls me Bjorn. They ascertained, together, that I hated those names. We watched tennis growing up.

I learned to take photos on a point-and-shoot. I learned only recently about light meters, about middle gray.

The inanimate objects are speaking: the damp towel darkening the back of the door. The coffee pot, empty, but still on. I walk outside to toss papers at the recycling bin. It is difficult to return to the quiet of where I live.

Older brother #1 calls, but I don't pick up. He reminds me not to miss Brother Two's birthday. He leaves the mathematician's number on the machine. No pressure, he says.

There is no surface I did not wash or vacuum when you left. Let me be clear here. Everything has been picked up, held, and replaced. It's not that everything was bad. I had been craving something. What you gave me was something. It felt, at the time, like something.

Chrissy, my brothers say: You should have more than just something.

When I was younger, I didn't know the language that contained Massapoag. Now I know: Algonquin. Back then, I looked where I always looked: the dictionary, World Books, the encyclopedia. Twenty years ago, books were school, mirror, portal: it was the only way to search or travel. I found this definition: *any of the hunted players in the children's game of cowboys and Indians.* But books are wrong, too: faulty maps drawn by people who want to set something straight. But it was never straight; it was crooked, shady. West Indian, East Indian, American Indian: all people named by people who were not Indian at all.

In the dictionary, there was also India ink, Indian path, Indian meal, and Indian yellow. The last was something my second brother would like: *an orange-yellow pigment obtained from the urine of cows fed on mango-leaves.* It would make him laugh. Think of mangoes. We are this kind of Indian, by which I mean East, but no one I know actually uses the term. East Indian. Who are these words for? *We know.*

I don't want you, now, to know anything real about me, but you know this: I hated to get off the phone with you. You said you knew I would immediately dial another number: Brothers One or Two or my mother. Anything to fill the space. Learn to live with it, you said. You are stronger, you said. You were leaving again for Chestnut Street.

She is the girl who frames photos of your sisters and your mother. She can group them on your bureau (the one you painted together) and three-two-one, one-two-three, one-three-two their order. She arranges your life. She can take photographs, fresh from the camera, from the night chemicals, and magnet them to the fridge, pin them to cork, leave them on the dashboard until they curl like canoes. These are the photos that belong. You record all the major holidays of the year. I always thought of her as your weekend. (I believed that I counted in your real life.) This is what I most regret.

I won't pick up my address book. I never called you back. I'm learning to play my CDs all the way through. It bothered you that I played so many songs on repeat.

For the first ten weeks after you left, I could sense times of day or night when you might also have been thinking of me. I could feel it—I was sure of this once or twice. But I can no longer feel what you are thinking. What might end up on a list you will make.

Whether you ever even told her. What you tell yourself: I have no idea.

Brother #2 says: Of course, he didn't tell her. Why would he tell her? He doesn't want to end up alone. Didn't we teach you anything? Never trust a guy.

But neither of my brothers ever met you, ever saw how you looked at the lake, ever heard how you pronounced Mass-a-po-ag, how you listened to my stories. Still: you have turned into what we always suspected: a ghost in a string of ghosts. A ghost with mediocre teeth and a good heart. A ghost with a weakness for girls with bright eyes and blurred edges. Predictable: a weakness for weak girls.

Maybe you have no need of a magic camera, of a way to record. How do you order your memory? How do you make your garden grow?

Maybe you think only of the girl on Chestnut Street. When you die, though, I will be a mourner at your wake. I think you would come to my wake also, partake in the cake, the yellow cake separating from frosting, the way I hear skin will pull away from bone. You will fork mouthfuls just to do something.

You will look at the blown-up photos, my unusually large teeth. You would look at the row of dolls I made of clothespins, acorns, and quilt scraps. You would see the family of Indians sitting to the side. You would say you were my friend. I would nudge the pink into your neck until finally you left for a cigarette and a magazine, a cigarette and a drive, a cigarette and a drink. You would shake my older brothers' hands. You would stand with my family, looking at my picture, and then this picture would help me go, release me from this spinning. By this time, when I am in the ground, only my molars will last, the metal fillings outlasting all skin; my hair and nails still growing, unable to stop.

This is a story about what will never happen. This is a story about things that never happened. Watch me annihilate you. There was no great fire, no plane crash. There was no wake, no crossing of rivers. We walk toward a mountain. We long for the curve in the road. We look at each other, heads leaning in. You are carrying a staff. The girl's face is happy. I could never see your face.

* * *

You were a book I misread. Perhaps you were the assailant (tall white male, half-day's growth, abused by your father, anger at the world), but I couldn't recognize you without the ski mask. I wanted you to be the one watching out for me. I didn't want to see what all the wise men and wiser women gently warned me about: You were one of many to keep watch for. What is it that the wise ones say: *Keep walking and you will avoid so much of this, you will find your way. You can walk away.* The elders are patient and they smile at me. The old ones raise their hands, a simultaneous greeting and farewell. Yes, I answer them. I will walk in well-lit areas. I will not walk alone.

I am the maiden, the lookout, the sentry. I am the only doll I must save in case of fire. I will stop-drop-and-roll. I will join my brothers outside. They will bridge their arms to steady me, they will finally get along. I will not be alone.

Even on the phone with my brothers, I start to hum, then sing. The CD wants to play the song all the way through, but why should any track end? All I have to do is dream and I can't stop myself from reaching back to press play again: from wanting the song to stay in that moment, that perfect pitch of longing.

Older Brother #2: Would you stop with the crappy music already?

When you are on Chestnut Street, or Avocado, or Citrus—or any of those fucking fruit streets—your eyes will mark the photo of the two of you on Fire Island from last summer or the summer before. Perhaps you will walk over to the bureau and pick up the photo, lightly tap the edges so that the picture is not crooked in the frame, so that it lies flat and it lies straight. You will hold it in your hands and then place it back on the dresser, not exactly over the dustless spot. I know you well enough to know that while you notice too much, you will not notice that.

This is the picture, which is framed. This is how I must think of you. Photos of us are spooled away, unexposed—I catch sight of them and their weak teeth at the edge of sleep. They smudge the edges of mirrors with their persistence, with their terrible vision of another way, with their unreasonable longing. And what state would that be? It's a photo overexposed—too much sunlight blinding us. After what is left pushes at us, beginning.

This is not the only story of what happened between us, but it is the only one I will tell.

What is the point of telling you that I still wake up remembering (as though you are here!) your childhood-blue eyes. How you used to look at me. As though you were waiting to hear whatever story might begin. *No one saves anyone.* As though you wanted to sit on my floor, tipping back bottles, draining bottles, collecting words and looking at me, for a very long time. As though you were more than unreliable teeth and heart. Your eyes, a kind of frame. My hands, enough. As though you had decided to stay.

Even now I hear my older brothers talking. *Hasn't she been listening to us? Move on, Chrissy. Stop perseverating.* And I want to tell them, I was listening all the time. I was watching you all the time. What girls are tossing their sheets, dreaming of your backs, thinking you will turn around, that you are not merely gathering your jackets and your wallets, that you are not merely preparing to walk away? You are just boys, walking. You were just a boy, walking. No one saves anyone.

Originally published in our Fall 2018 issue, *Edges*

---

on following pages, selections from

The Proscenium

Vi Khi Nao

3. PREFACE:

"At first, she[1] tries to carry the purse. She tries to insert the entire alphabet[2] into her purse[3]. At first, she tries to insert[4]..." – Ambrosio LeAbsence

---

1

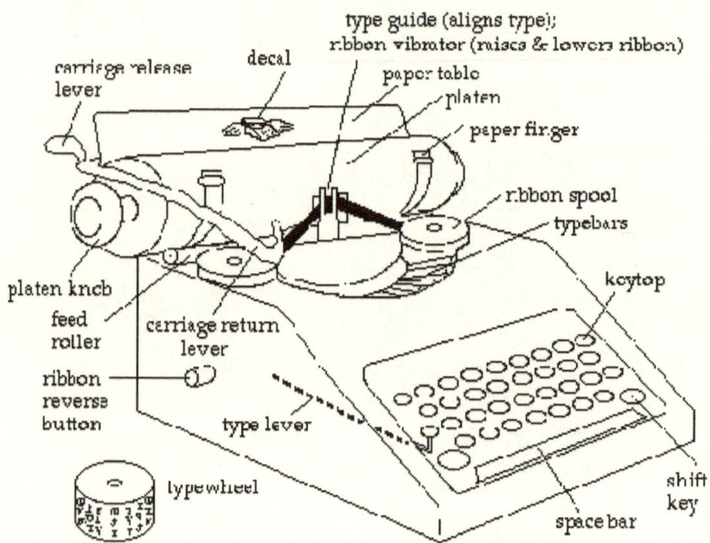

[2] Valance is in her bedroom. After taking the typewriter to her bed, Valance takes apart the typewriter. She unlatches the carriage release lever, decal, platen knob, feed roller, ribbon reverse button, carriage

return lever, type lever, space bar, shift keys, keytops, ribbon spools, paper finger, platen, paper table, ribbon vibrator, type guide, little bolts, and parts, and inserts them into a Christofle bread bag. She keeps the typebars, not in the bag, closer to her body. Valance lines the typefaces on the edge of the bed—in white cotton sheets. She enters the bathroom. In the bathroom, she grips the oval, stainless steel bowl and turns the hot water spigot. When the water reaches ¾ full, she grabs a hand towel from the handle, turns the spigot to the left, and returns to the bed with the handheld items. She sits next to the bed and places the oval bowl on the bed and dips the towel into the bowl and wrenches it so that the towel acts as an oshibori. She begins to wash each typebar with the oshibori. Splotches of ink begin to occupy the towel's terrycloth composition. She places each typebar on the bed along its edge like an assembly line. When she places each typebar down, the typebar creates a darker halo around the typebars on the cotton sheet as the cotton sheet tries to absorb the water and the light weight of the typebars. She rubs the ink off the semicolon, colon, numbers, and quotation marks. When they are desiccated of their printed literary history, Valance assembles the washed typebars in the QWERTY panel as seen in the diagram on the other page (ignoring the typewheel) with the letters of the typebars turning toward her body so that she may see the letters protrude on the spring steel before her. Valance lets the air drink in the last microscopic water residue from the typebars and walks toward her drawers. She unrolls a 6 x 6 foot white Ingres sheet and walks the paper to the wall that faces the foot of the bed. She picks up the roll of white artist tape from the birch floor. With her left shoulder and lower torso holding the sheet to the wall, she begins to tear approximately seven pieces of tape (each four inches) and dabs them makeshiftingly to the Ingres. They hold the Ingres to the wall without her support. Then, she begins to tear one six foot tape from the artist roll four times and slowly tapes the Ingres along its edges and sides. She walks to her drawer and pulls out a colossal C-Thru Compass. Gripping the knee-action bow compass, she walks back to the hung Ingres and circles the 0.5 mm mechanical pencil on the Ingres paper. Satisfied with the circular four foot diameter drawing on Ingres, she drops the compass on the floor, returns to her bed, undresses until she is nude, and lies down.

$

AMBROSIO: **I have watched her for so long from the window with a stack of three milk crates beneath me. My sister, the poet. *(On the exterior of the window, Ambrosio***

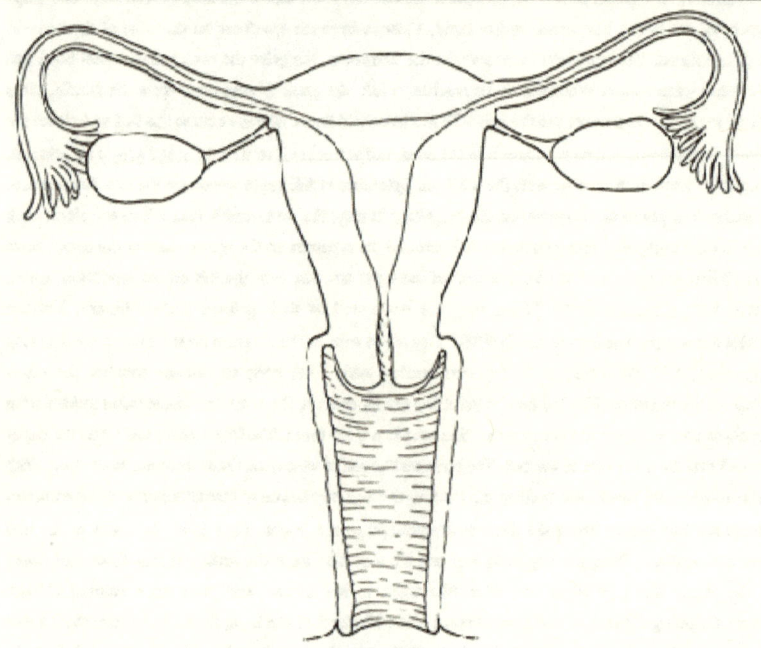

[4] Ping Pong tournaments exist in some brothels in Thailand. These purse holders enter the entertainment facilities to exercise their purses' rights and act as participants in the ritual of human rights conflicts. Some have held chopsticks without hands and have been able to grab grapes, tofu, mango slices, and feed customers Pad Thai noodles regularly. A fancy type of fine dining and recreation of infertility. Valance is not a purse holder. She is a poet.

10th Anniversary Issue
Author Comments

Vi Khi Nao on "The Proscenium"

Tell us about your process for this piece.

I wanted to write a novel about a woman who uses her uterus to type her novel. Her vaginal's typewriter typebars would be ejected/disembogued from her genital wall onto a sheet of paper. The "author" wrote/finished the novel, but that novel only had three letters (the article): T H E. This is an excerpt of my progress with the book. I titled the thing "The Proscenium" because the typebars on a typewriter resembles the stage of an antique theater, where dramatic performances can live their lives fully on the histrionic imagination of the reader or on the page itself.

Originally published in our Fall 2013 Issue, *The Fiction Issue*

Time Served

Celeste Prince

On Mondays through Fridays and the occasional Saturday, we are registered nurses, yoga instructors, hairstylists and teachers. At work we wear plastic badges pinned to lapels with our names—Nika, Katherine, Chantal, Trudy—and smile without showing our teeth. After hours we are unabashed shower singers, occasional gourmet cooks, sheepish crime show addicts and avoiders of dish duty. Today, we are also girlfriends to men behind bars. We sit in stained, blue plastic chairs in different corners of the city jail waiting room, thankful we left our name-tags at home.

When we each arrived at the courthouse, sweat tickling our scalps as it dried in the air conditioning, an older security guard greeted us before we could whisper our questions. "He's over there, sugar," he said, smiling, pointing back to a tan brick building next door—as if he already knew who we were.

But that's the problem. The labels on our purses, the careful strokes of our eyeliner, and the pulled, pinched pout of our mouths all say that we are not supposed to be here. This is an error. We slow down for emergency vehicles. We pay our gym membership dues on time. We take out our IDs when asked and answer questions from men wearing gold badges with a pleasant "Yes, sir" and "Absolutely not, sir."

Yet we are here and it's as if our names are written on the books too.

* * *

I want to say I haven't slept, that I don't plan to close my eyes until Jarvis comes home.

That I sat up all night with a vigil of candles and incense on the coffee table, hands clasped in distressful prayer. But we were in the middle of the silent treatment, so when Jarvis still hadn't returned from his night economics class, I put away the newest *Food and Wine* magazine, locked the door and took advantage of the extra space in the bed. He probably went out for wings with friends, I thought, and in the morning I would find him on the couch, his drool puddle smelling of mesquite, eyes bleary and unapologetic.

The collect call came an hour later, the line full of static. "Jarvis Green," I heard him say, his voice like a child exhausted from play, followed by the operator: "an inmate at the City of Houston jail..." and suddenly the room felt very, very warm.

Movies forget to tell real people that cellphones can't accept collect calls, so instead of an explanation, I was left with silence. When I found his online rap sheet, his freedom added up to four digits. First charge: parking violation from last year, before he sold his car to buy an XBox. I remember that ticket. We had parked downtown without paying the hopper, thinking it was free, and came back from the gym to a smirking meter maid.

"I don't need trouble today," the attendant said. He rested a hand on the bulge in his back pocket and repeated himself until we got in the car.

Second charge: missed court date. Likely because he didn't pay the first ticket. Third charge: additional missed court date. I don't understand the wording of the fourth charge but the city still wants money for it. Petty crimes worth one thousand dollars total, more than twice our rent.

For almost nine months we've been playing house since my parents moved back to Barbados, but it's nothing in the June Cleaver sense. We shop for groceries apart, the different containers in the cabinets and fridge covered in neon Post-Its with our names scribbled in capital letters. Jarvis' PowerAde and bologna, my Greek yogurt and granola. We greet each other with subtle nods instead of moist pecks on the cheek. Some weekends I scrub the kitchen until the tile squeaks and on the first of every month I tuck a money order for him under the coffee maker.

Sometimes, though, during the night, in the bed we share, his hand brushes the V-line between my hip and thigh and I turn into his arms soundlessly, eager to pull him close. It is a quiet agreement that would confuse most except Jarvis, and he is its greatest defender.

"When you say things like that, it reminds me why you're not my gal," he said weeks before he became an inmate, when I groaned about his phone vibrating after twelve. Who the hell, I wondered aloud into my pillow, needed to get a hold of him this late? Was he so popular that it couldn't wait until morning? My voice arched into the whine of an ignored preschooler. He counter-attacked: nagging, he said, is something a girlfriend does. Jarvis didn't use such labels, thus voiding my complaint.

A car's brakes squealed outside and I braced for the sound of an impact.

When nothing happened I rolled over to face him.

"Three years later and I'm still a name on the list?"

Three years of driving him to job interviews, of his friends calling me the wrong name and laughing off the mistake, of elementary yet seductive late night text messages from his phone ("Girl stop playin u kno u want me btwn ur legs rite now"), of knowing I was one and not The One.

I pushed on: "Trudy penciled right after Marsha, Megan and Molly?"

Briefly the other women appeared in a sophisticated mental slideshow, their pictures and stats cycling by, each more sultry and exciting than her predecessor. Taryn: brunette, songwriter, likes Pilates and red velvet cake. Stella: strawberry-blonde, dreamt of becoming an EMT, current lingerie sales rep.

"Please, who's named Marsha anymore?" The mattress bounced as Jarvis laughed at his joke, missing my glare in the darkness. "You see anybody else in my bed?" He kissed my neck in a soft line sloping towards by ribs. "Just you, girl. Just True."

Tonight, sure, I thought. But while I'm at the school, reprimanding sophomores for forgetting their vocabulary homework, or before my clothes took up half his closet—who then? Once, while he was out, I thought I smelled a perfume I didn't own on the pillows. One second and I couldn't find the spot again, yet my hands shook for hours as I lay there, alone, thinking *who, who, who besides True.*

"Anyway, that possession shit is tired," Jarvis continued. "All that 'he's mine, she's mine, who you talking to, where you been' nonsense. Other people jumping in the business like it's a public swimming pool."

He sighed as if to reserve a moment of silence for the unhappy couples arguing in their homes right then, spreading out stacks of hotel receipts and call logs on the coffee table before their partners like a jigsaw puzzle they hesitated to solve.

"That doesn't happen with you and me. Outside of here"—the mattress shook again with his circular gestures, indicating the bedroom—"I'm Jarvis, you're Trudy. Independent. Unlabeled. I know I'm with you but I don't go around telling folks. That's private, right?"

It was a question, but there was no lilt at the end that signaled I could agree, protest, or ask for an explanation. Two chilled fingers lifted the elastic of my panties and dove under the cotton. My head emptied. I forgot my witty line comparing unlabeled men to items missing price tags: people just assume they're free for the taking. Another time, I thought, as I lifted my face to brush his lips.

The phone buzzed again; the table clock read 12:41.

"So what are we doing?" I asked. "What is this called?" The cords of my body were coiled too tight, aching to stretch somewhere stable. I needed a definition, any word that would make me more than another warm mass in his bed.

Another sigh, a heavy draw inward: he was annoyed. "Just cool out, True." His shadowed head dipped towards the foot of the bed. "What, you don't wanna be here anymore?"

There it was; he didn't say it but the word enveloped the room: *Leave.*

It was a threat loaded with promise for both of us. If I packed up, he would have to move or find someone else to share his apartment with, and I would be on the street. And then—would we still be friends or lovers? Strangers? I wasn't ready to consider it.

Before I could speak, his tongue—flat, long, penetrating, insistent—interrupted my thoughts. Typical. If the conversation isn't going his way, Jarvis finds a different route.

Months ago when I came to Jarvis crying about my parents' move and he handed me my key as if it were a lost earring, I saw the exchange as a sign of our friendship, our casual comfort with each other: satisfied without cause for extra commotion. Yet when I woke in the hushed apartment alone, light gathered in unusual corners and hiding from others, I felt like a hung-over guest in a stranger's motel room.

* * *

Minutes build into hours. The lobby feels like a pressure cooker. I gnash my gum and glare. I have a degree, dammit. Someone like me isn't supposed to be here. I tried to put this in my tone when I first talked to the officers, but they just told me to take a seat. With a glance around the room, though, I could guess the same thoughts had gone through the other women's minds when they arrived. It doesn't matter who I was before – I'm here now. Without my consent, I am just like all of these women: startled, anxious, fearing the unknown, trembling with wordless anger.

As we wait for updated news about our lesser halves, our muscles seize from the strain of keeping our great—not just good—shoes off the urine-smelling tile. Kat's are especially fabulous: tangerine peep-toes in a size that only elves could make.

Nika shakes her head. "Girl, I couldn't wear those in the ER."

"Present from my husband," Kat says. She swings her legs. "Pinch like hell, though."

At work our roles are easy; here, we don't know our lines. Every slam of a door, every loud shout in the hallway makes us jump, thinking *Now, that's him coming now.* But nobody's man appears and the officers' lazy reply of "wait 'til after the shift change" to our questions isn't enough. Our feet aren't hurting any less, so we cheat.

With a gold-polished fingernail, Chantal beckons us to follow her to the restroom down the hall. Inside the floor is wet and three of the four stalls are missing toilet paper. I make a silent promise to will away any desire to pee until I get home.

"Do what I do," Chantal says.

We spend a half hour pinching our cheeks, biting our tongues and pulling out eyelashes until salt-water clumps the mascara. If the makeup streaked, our anguish would be more convincing, but alas, we bought it before we were cast as The Down Ass Chick, unaware we might have to challenge Halle Berry's Oscar acceptance tears.

Earlier while I got dressed at home after calling for a sub, I turned on the radio. On the local hip-hop station, the DJ looped songs where rappers praised their ride-or-die girlfriends, ladies who stood by their men, no question, even taking the fall during run-ins with cops. None of these ultra-women had a problem slipping a loaded artillery weapon into her Hermès purse in case shit got real at the movie theater. This, the stereo seemed to advise, is who I needed to emulate: The Down Ass Chick. They are tough—carved from the ribs of their suitors but with legs and asses that make other, lesser men wipe their mouths in disbelief.

Why had I never met these women? Surely we must have passed each other in the dairy aisle at Kroger. Still, I felt inspired—a chance to prove to Jarvis that I deserve the pronoun *we.* I grabbed my checkbook and hooked on my pushup bra. An officer might need extra incentive to let Jarvis slide, I thought as I adjusted the girls in the mirror.

Now, under the off-white fluorescent bathroom bulbs, I feel like a fraud.

Chantal wets a paper towel and dabs our cheeks. "Need to look like we've been crying," she explains. "Like, bawling so hard we threw up." She blinks rapidly as she works. "There, look at you now." We turn to examine the damage, and the dirty mirrors reflect four confused women who walked into the wrong audition.

Regardless, we parade triumphant back to Officer Vargas, the desk sergeant. "Any word?" we say, hopeful this display of despair might inspire a new answer. We think we are slick. Nika works a real tear down her jawline. "How much longer?" we ask. "Is there anything I can do? Should do?"

Officer Vargas adjusts her bifocals and smiles—or is it a smirk? "Cute, ladies." She shakes her head behind the bulletproof glass. "No, nothing yet," she says. "Hang tight, sweetheart."

It's recycled, but her sympathy feels original. Our chests contract. We resist the urge to reach through the opening in the glass and squeeze her hand.

Beside her, an antiquated computer monitor details in green text our beloveds' offenses and the hefty fines to be paid. Two hundred and fifty dollars for a missed court date, when the one moronic parking ticket would have been thirty-five bucks. The descriptions are written in a code we—women like us—never had to learn: numbers next to a string of consonants, abbreviations, words like "warrant" and "fine" that don't bring a clear picture to the mind's eye. The only phrase we recognize is "failure to appear in court."

Yes, we think, *failure* is definitely the operative word.

* * *

Officer Vargas says we can confront the ones who dragged us away from our Wednesday afternoon routines at four o' clock. It is twenty to three. Chantal has been here since ten. Nika posted bail at noon. Kat and I checked in after one. Nobody came dressed for such a long visit. It's too cold for two of us, too warm for the rest, and nervous sweat makes it impossible for us to share sweaters. We've spent less time at the mall looking for boots and at least then there's an end reward, even if it's just a pretzel from Auntie Anne's.

To keep from staring down the clock, we talk. At first in frightened chirps (*I wish I knew everything was okay. Why won't someone tell me what's happening?*) and then deeper cutting tones (*This is what I get for letting that fool back in my house. Calling himself a man. If he was such a man he wouldn't be in here*). Here, we do not have to pretend that this is an exciting adventure. It's just us. The affirmation gained by tearing the men down allows us to scoot closer, putting away our magazines and phones to look at each other. Each concealed face reveals the same trepidation rippling under the lip-gloss, rouge and foundation. We want them to walk through the doors, unchained, but don't know if they will be the same ones we wanted before, and if they are not, if we will still want them at all.

Nika found Warren's toothbrush still dry after she woke up. "I knew he was either in jail," she says, "or in the morgue." According to Officer Vargas, Warren was caught driving with an expired license, something she didn't know until this morning, in addition to some missed speeding tickets. Off the record, there is a whisper that he wasn't alone when the police pulled him over. Livid isn't a big enough word to describe her feelings.

"He's been driving my car for months, looking for a job," she moans. Her pearl pink scrubs are freshly pressed, her braids pulled back. She glances at her phone several times as she talks. "I thought about not even coming down here to get him. But then he'll miss another day of work tomorrow and that can't happen."

Warren is not hers; her fingernail underlines the air to solidify her point. She hesitates when she sees our confusion. He stays at her house, in a separate bedroom, she explains, because they have a son together. Nika discovered she was pregnant a month after they broke up. His name is Shane. The picture of him eating animal crackers on her keychain makes us all coo. He's two years old and at day care, and if Warren isn't released before five, Nika will have to pay overtime for picking the boy up late on top of the bail money she already spent.

Looking at Nika is like staring at a mirror, the opposite and the same.

I'm too curious to be polite. "Why do you stay with him?" I ask. "Wouldn't it be easier to just break it off?" They are questions I've asked myself, but my answers feel cliché, like I am too weak to trust being on my own.

Behind her glasses Nika's eyes appear wide and wet. "I only put up with this because my son needs a father," she says. "I'm woman enough to admit that I can't do it alone." She purses her lips. "But maybe I've been alone this whole time."

* * *

Chantal witnessed her boyfriend's arrest outside of the Whataburger a few blocks from her house. "Public urination," she says and tries to laugh. We have trouble smiling. "He didn't want to wait to go inside with me. He wasn't wearing a shirt, so they slapped on public indecency too."

Darnell is twenty-five, thirteen years younger than Chantal, and has already proposed to her. Twice. The night he was arrested he had planned on the third as a charm when nature called; Chantal had glimpsed the ring in his pocket when police searched him in the parking lot.

"He's not ready to be a husband." She waves her arms at the waiting room. "Case in point."

In between prattling about their May-December romance and the struggle for a blessing from his skeptical family, Chantal shows us the deodorant and fresh shirt she brought for Darnell when he gets out. Hers is love, full and fierce despite the circumstances. She's not a wife or mother yet but it's a role we can tell she's been studying.

She keeps saying, "The last time," and I think, *So this ain't her first rodeo.* A glance at the others confirms our mutual ponderings. Will this, too, be our fate, spending more afternoons in this replicated room? It's hard to imagine. Jarvis is the opposite of a seasoned felon. He supervises the morning warehouse crew at IKEA while taking two night classes at the community college. He trims his beard before and after work, tweezing out stray hairs that his razor won't catch. The sun doesn't set on Jarvis' five o' clock shadow. I doubt he is enduring his lock-up with grace.

A door squeaks open somewhere in the building and we all flinch but no one appears.

"You know," Chantal says, "he's not even my type? I've never been with a guy like him."

We clap our hands and shake our fingers at each other. We were just thinking the same thing. Nika likes academics, Kat won't date anyone who doesn't go to church or the gym, and Chantal usually gravitates toward professionals, like the oil executives in suits who walk by her Midtown salon. The men locked somewhere inside this building don't have private offices or own three-piece suits. Sitting in this lobby, it doesn't feel like they ever will.

I've played the no-label game with Jarvis for so long I've forgotten my type. The only men I meet these days are the parents of my students during conferences. "English teachers never looked like you back in the day," some might say, after I've told them their child has a fifth grade reading level in high school. "If I were Nicholas, I'd be too distracted to read properly too." Sometimes the single (or not) dads offer dinner as we shake hands goodbye, and I say no. Jarvis shakes his head whenever I tell him, but he's just like them, imagining the prim schoolteacher crawling toward them across a bearskin rug.

I tell the other women and they laugh. We all met these men who see our jobs as a vehicle for their fantasy. They wanted to see Kat practice downward dog in their bedrooms or have Nika take their temperature wearing nothing but a stethoscope. But in the morning they didn't want to rub our feet, swollen from standing for ten hours, or make us coffee and listen while we talked about the client who paid with a bad check. They instead dropped us off at our doorsteps, and a day later sent texts saying how great the other night was while asking for risqué camera phone pictures in our prescribed uniforms.

We deleted the messages and went to work.

* * *

A few weeks ago on my way to work a guy on the light rail asked for my phone number. As we approached the Medical Center he appeared in front of my seat, smiling. "I've been trying to make eye contact with you for three stops," he said. "Now I have to get off or I'll be late."

I hadn't noticed. My newest commuter novel kept me re-reading sentences seven times before I could figure out the dense vocabulary. I wasn't sure if I hadn't missed my own stop. As I looked up I realized the stranger wasn't just some dude trying out a line but a Professional Man, clean shaven in gray scrubs and no visible tattoos – likely the subject of many a nurse's work crush, and he was talking to me. Instead of replying like a coquette, I gaped at him.

"So would it be a waste of time," he continued, "to ask for your number, before I leave?"

Jarvis' face crossed my mind for less than a second. "No." I even volunteered to type it into his phone, not expecting more than a story for me to tell the other older English teachers during lunch—a chance to gloat for fifteen minutes and then return to grading reading quizzes.

I couldn't help it. The students bombed their reading quiz, and I needed to take out the frustration. "Someone wanted my number today," I told Jarvis later that night. He was watching ESPN in the living room, legs spread long and wide across the couch cushions. I stood in the kitchen, barefoot in a pair of his sweats, balancing my checkbook. My hair, still damp from the shower, dripped occasional spots on the counter.

"Why, to tutor their kid?"

"For a date." I turned to face him. "A guy on the train. He works at one of the hospitals."

He didn't look away from the TV. "What for?"

"I know you heard me." My hands were shaking. He kept his arms crossed, the highlights flickering across his slacken face. "What do you think about that? If someone else asked me out?"

"True, I told you what it is."

He rolled over on to his stomach as if he was done talking but it looked too much like surrender. I wanted a fight, a tussle, a battle over me like the drama of Camelot that my freshmen were slowly trying to read. I walked over to the couch and shoved his legs to the floor. "That's all? You wouldn't be mad?"

He sighed with his eyes closed. "You want me to jump up and down like an asshole, talk about how you only belong to me and I'll kill any fool who wants to step in? That's not how this works, True. I thought you wanted to avoid that tired shit. I know I do."

He wasn't going to give me what I wanted. I abandoned the game and traded in talking for touching. In the bedroom his goatee, freshly cut and coarse, rubbed against my shoulder until the skin prickled.

"Bend back a little," he dictated while he gently pressed my hands to the wall. There was extra gravel in his voice. "Does that feel good? Do you like that?"

I didn't answer, but he finished without seeming to notice.

* * *

Kat appears young but is the only one with a ring and a fresh burgundy bruise creeping from under her shirt collar. She says little about her situation. The secrets her petite body must hold, we wonder. We only know that she teaches yoga and sells houses, her man's name is Thomas, and their downstairs neighbor called the cops on him this morning.

The whispers she and Officer Vargas exchange sound more urgent than our boyfriends' stupid problems. "It's up to you, honey," Vargas repeats. Kat bites her lip and asks for more time to think. It takes a collective summons of strength to keep from asking, "Think about *what*?"

We're distracted by a woman in khakis and a faded green polo rapping on the office glass. She points to a young boy on the other side, standing with a few other inmates. "Sign the release paper, dammit," she hollers.

"I gotta go to work. Stop playing."

A few officers stand inside the office watching, waiting. The boy shakes his head and says something we can't hear. A male cop interprets: "He says he'll just stay here and serve the time."

The woman growls. Her nametag says "Paula," but her posture and the bags under her eyes say Mother. Her purse looks second-hand, the leather strap clinging to the buckle. Her shoes are scuffed and worn. "That's that jail talk. I already paid his bail. I know y'all don't give refunds." She bangs a fist on the counter and presses her face to the glass to look at her son. He can't be older than sixteen. "Boy, come out of there. Sign the paper so I can take you home." Her voice catches, cracks then resurges stronger. "Let's. Go."

The boy keeps shaking his head until the woman stomps out of the room cursing. For a minute it's quiet, and then we suck our teeth and scowl at the boy, but he has already turned back to his new friends.

* * *

When the women look at me, I shrug. "We're not really together," I say. "At least, that's what he says." Unlike my parents and co-workers, they nod instead of furrowing their brows.

As far as why he's here, Officer Vargas told me Jarvis had a warrant for his arrest because of the tickets, and last night he was picked up somehow. "Wrong place, wrong time," she explained. "Maybe a friend got pulled over, and they ran everyone's IDs. I see it a lot. Folks go months without knowing the police are looking for them and then one day, you drive too fast by a cop and bang! Everything catches up to you."

"Does it feel like love?" Chantal asks.

"Who can think about love in this room?" Nika grumbles. "Love gave me stretch marks and a toddler pretending to be a grown-ass man."

Kat cackles and rubs the mark on her neck.

Chantal waves Nika off. "Does it?" she asks again. She leans toward me, her fingers gripping the arms of her chair. "You said it's been three years. That's *gotta* feel like love to you, honey."

"Don't be so sure," Kat says.

But Chantal wants to know. She looks like my students when I pass back their graded papers, so earnest and hopeful yet dreading what I might say. I tell her yes, it feels like love, just so she'll smile, but she probably knows it's a lie.

I scratch a mosquito bite on my ankle. "I don't know why he called me, though," I say. "I'm not his girl, so why bother."

I expect laughter and cosigning, but they frown. Of course he called you, they say. Was he supposed to call Tyrone or some other no-count homeboy instead? Hell no. We—the women—always know what to do. We are prepared for these types of emergencies. It's been built into us by God Himself. I can't tell if this is what they believe, or if they've been listening to the same songs on the radio.

* * *

Three-ten. The mood needs to lighten. Nika tries to joke and we join in, planning the abuse we will unleash on the men as soon as we get a few blocks away from the jail. "Don't want to be brought back ten minutes later," we giggle.

A buzzer sounds, and a door unlocks. We freeze mid-snicker, eyes on the release gate. A teenager with a box haircut in a dirty Texans jersey shuffles out. None of ours, but we watch him anyway. The boy could be our kid brother, a cousin, a mentee from the Boys and Girls Club. Not old enough to earn the cooled spot next to us in our beds but bold enough to lick his lips as we pass him on the street. There is a jaunt in his step when he notices the audience in the waiting room. He loudly tells Officer Vargas that he wants to make a call, and she directs him to the pay phone with a flicked wrist. Searching for a coin, the boy pats his pockets and the possessions returned to him in a plastic Ziploc. Train ticket stub, two cigarettes, a bobby pin—no money. He turns to the women in waiting and meets our eyes.

"'Ey ladies," he says and smiles. His teeth are tiny.

Ignoring him is as easy as breathing.

"How y'all doing?"

What kind of answer does he expect? Inane questions deserve inane responses. We're doing fine today, just waiting for our men to quit joking around and come out of there, so we can go to the grocery store and the laundromat, because we're out of spaghetti and clean underwear. But *we're* being selfish. How are *you*, sugar?

"Fine," someone replies.

"Wondering if someone could help me out."

Before he begins his next sentence, his face registers our fury, guesses at the rage that will spill from our Revlon lips if he foolishly asks for a quarter. One more thing for us to give up for a man. We will rip his jersey through the middle, cleaving the seven from the two, our French tips transformed into poisoned claws. He will become a sacrifice, the goat roasted on the spit of our discontent, an appetizer until the real offenders are released into our care again.

Or maybe that's not what this churning toxic feeling looks like. Maybe it looks like an untouched dinner plate in the microwave. Hair in rollers and plaits while eyes flick between the silent phone and the crime dramas on TV. Sweat and coconut grease sliding down the neck until the phone finally rings with an automated recording confirming the worst.

Maybe it's a longing for familiar calloused hands gripping hips. Hushed instructions. The occasional smack or bite. A designated towel to cover the wet spot on the sheets.

It doesn't matter. Whatever its name or how it looks, it feels like a vomited meal that's been reheated and fed back to us with a knife and fork.

Chantal pulls out a quarter from her wallet. "Here you go, baby," she says. "I know your mama wants to know where you are."

Of us she is the eldest, one faint gray hair winking from her bob, her purse more sensible without an obvious label stamped all over the fabric. Eldest and yet this doesn't stop us from glaring at her when the boy grins, says, "Yes, ma'am" and, using her donated coin, calls up a person who answers to the moniker "shorty" then saunters outside to await his ride. Chantal, wise and humble, avoids our eyes.

After he leaves, we subside into silence. Our Girls Club is too fragile. One man's presence, the mere scent of the danger between his thighs that controls more of our actions than we like to admit, is enough to turn us into strangers again. Nika checks her voice mail. I wish for the nth time that I brought a book to read. Kat examines a hangnail. Chantal looks like she wants to talk more, or scream, or weep. She instead adjusts her belt on her dress and gets up to ask Officer Vargas for another update.

* * *

In our separate corners, we chew the cud of our anger slowly, when a tall blonde in pumps enters the room. Her outfit looks like mourning clothes from Neiman Marcus. All of a sudden, we feel much less glamorous in the face of her authentic shoulder bag. Officer Vargas and she chat for a few moments. She is told the same as us: visitation at four, possible release around five, charges and fines may apply. "So I just pay over there?" the woman asks, pointing behind her. "And he'll be out?" She is already reaching for her wallet as if money could solve these problems. Vargas told us earlier to keep our pocketbooks closed. The more time these men served, the less they owed in fines. By the time they are released, she says, the city may just ask for some community service hours instead of cash. It's not the money they should worry about, though, but what other things they will need to repay when they finally walk out.

The blonde's hand trembles as she brushes some lint from her blouse.

Even with her Louis Vuitton checkbook cover she's like us – frightened and full of questions. But as soon as Vargas finishes giving her instructions concerning bail, she clicks back outside. We cut looks at each other.

"She seemed in a hurry," Chantal says.

"Late for her spin class," I say.

We dissolve into laughter, improper and loud. Nika howls behind her hand and Chantal's shoulders bounce. My stomach cramps. Kat holds her face, torso bent towards her lap. It takes a moment for us to see if she's joined in the joke or succumbed to a greater grief. Minutes ago she signed a sheet of paper then disappeared into a back room with an officer we didn't recognize. She returned with puffy eyes, hands clenched into fists.

When she lifts her head, Officer Vargas calls her name. She's taken off her glasses.

"They're taking him to county, honey," she says.

Kat nods as if she understands but her body stiffens. The mark on her neck turns violet.

"It's been a long day. You should go home and rest."

"By myself?" Kat asks, her voice a whisper.

Another policewoman offers to drive her home. Kat gathers her things and gives us each a smile. "Alright, ladies," she says. Her drawl makes me smile weakly. She slides a white Chanel bag onto her shoulder and fixes her side ponytail. "Be good."

We mumble a stunned goodbye as she leaves. Chantal makes the sign of the cross and murmurs, "Bless her, Lord." To us, she says, "County means she's pressing charges on the bastard for knocking her around. They're transferring him to Harris County jail with all the other fuck-ups." She smiles at her curse. Nika and I murmur, "Amen."

* * *

Ten minutes to four, Vargas calls us to the desk. It's visitation time. Nika opts to stay behind. Warren doesn't expect her to be here and she wants him to stay ignorant for a little longer. Chantal and I fill out the forms to go upstairs. Name, age, driver's license number. I hesitate at a box asking for my relation to the inmate. Chantal puts "fiancée" on hers with a flourish. "Friend" doesn't fill up the space like "girlfriend" does but my current location makes me too nervous to lie.

I put "roommate." It fits just right.

The visitation room needs a makeover. Thick layers of yellow, flaking paint cover the steel walls, counter and stools. It looks just like TV but on an alternate level of awful. There is a phone receiver and a small glass window, just big enough for us to see the inmates' eyes.

"Should we pray?" asks Chantal. I'm too jarred by the swift change in scenery to say anything but yes. We hold hands and bow heads, asking God to help our men become the men we need them to be. "May they learn from all of this," Chantal pleads, "and return to Your brighter path, Lord." We're interrupted by fists banging on the wall. Jarvis' gray eyes squint through the inch-wide window.

"True," he says softly. "I didn't think I'd see you here, girl."

His voice, defeated and tired, unlocks something and I'm crying for real, salty snot running down my throat, eyes aflame. I use the edge of my tank top to wipe my nose. Next to me, Chantal pushes her gold fingers to the glass. She smiles as she talks to Darnell, and I cry harder because she looks so happy, as if the past cluster of hours happened in a dream. This is the end, I think. In an hour when they let our men go, I will have to do the same. It's been a long day. I look at Jarvis.

"I've been here," I say. "God, have I been here."

10th Anniversary Issue
Author Comments

Celeste Prince on "Time Served"

What do you remember about working on this piece?

My story was a way of working through the confusion of young, dumb relationships. When I wrote this piece, I was twenty-something years old and hustling through my MFA program. Each week, I would attend three-hour classes where my professors presented me with order and structure, then rush through Houston traffic to work at the downtown YMCA front desk where I gossiped with my coworkers about our messy love lives. Ghosting, catfishing, situationships -- so many specific terms for such fluid experiences. At the same time, my then live-in boyfriend was briefly arrested, and I woke up questioning everything I thought I knew about him and our relationship. All together, these situations fell so far outside of my comfort zone and my insular suburban childhood. What to do? Write about it. While my life looks dramatically different now than it did ten years ago when I wrote "Time Served," I still recognize the emotions I tried to verbalize. It's a beautiful memorial, in my opinion, to the uncertainty and certainty of youth.

Originally published in our Fall 2014 Issue, *Kianny Antigua*

Dalila

Kianny Antigua

Translated by Noah T. Myers from Spanish

After the divorce, I decided to move as far as I could from that bustling city, so full of him. I closed my eyes, pointed to a random spot on the map, and with my meager savings and everything I could stuff in the trunk, I hit the road.

I spent the first few days in a motel. Once I found a job waiting tables, I rented a room in the house of Mrs. Paula. The place wasn't big, but I didn't need much; what mattered to me was that I could relax and be alone.

Mrs. Paula had a son in his early twenties. He was tall with brown skin and a round, pleasant face, like a tomato from a TV ad. His name was Isidro, but for some odd reason, his mother called him Isidoro of Guatemala. When I asked Isidro the reason why, he responded, "at this point, not even she knows." It turned out that Mrs. Paula suffers from Alzheimer's, but by the time I found out it was too late: I had already gained an affection for her son and for my new flower, Dalila.

Cuscuta prunus is the scientific name of my dear Dalila, the name Isidro gave her. She is a mix of a parasitic flower and a vine that grows out of rocky outcrops, or, in the case of Dalila, out of the wall of my room. She is a radiant pink, almost fuchsia tone with long yellow stamens that she uses to move around and to show affection. Her stem is long, fine and so flexible it seems to be made of rubber, which is what gives her such ease of movement.

Isidro, who is a writer, says she's an extremely exotic specimen, "one in a million." He was the one who stopped me from hysterically ripping her out of the wall when I first discovered her, newly sprouted, winding around herself like a shiny little spider. He immediately named her and explained all the things I should know about her and how fortunate I was to have her. Little by little, I became attached to her— how could I not, really? She's so smart and sweet-natured. When I get home, no matter how late, her shining yellow stamens greet me with joy, waiting to be caressed. She climbs up into the crack between the rustic wall and the ceiling and waits, bubbly and glowing, for me to open the door and turn on the light, and then jumps onto my face, running through my hair and neck like scurrying ants. Isidro says she may be drawn to the smell of food that lingers on me. Later, I shower and get into bed, and when I turn off the light she curls up like spaghetti on a fork and goes to sleep.

This had been our routine for several months, but yesterday, when I got home, I found her in a nervous, frightened state. She wasn't waiting for me. This caught me off guard and I immediately became concerned. When I came into the bedroom and turned on the light, I found her winding around herself like a madwoman, like a clock with a hand trying to detach itself. Then she jumped toward me and her trembling tentacles first got tangled in my hair and then clasped tightly around my neck.

As late as it was, Isidro was still awake. Writing, he said. After helping to free my head from Dalila's grip, he explained what had transpired:

"Mom had a really long, intense attack. I had to give her a shot and take her to the doctor."

He told me that for a long period of time Mrs. Paula had not recognized him and because of that she had panicked and began throwing everything she could find at poor Isidro: plates, cups, pots, knives. Despondent and with his eyes clouding up, he showed me a bandage on his arm where the blade of one of the knives had reached him.

Now I understood why Dalila had been so afraid; poor thing, she wasn't born to deal with this kind of upheaval.

I spent another while talking with Isidro and then he went to finish the story he had been working on, something about a person who turns into a cockroach, or a cockroach that thought it was a person; I wasn't really sure.

Once I was in bed and sensing that Dalila had calmed down, I turned out the light and reflected on what had happened. It wasn't right to keep exposing Dalila to this type of convulsions; that would be inhumane. Mrs. Paula's disease was incurable and now she would have to be cared for by a nurse every day, according to Isidro. In other words, there would be no more privacy in the house. The solution would be for me to move. I had already saved up enough money to get an apartment, but one thing Isidro had told me was to never try to transplant Dalila; that would kill her. I had even considered cutting out a chunk of the wall so I could take her with me to a new home.

It was a rough, drowsy night. Now and then I would drift off, only to awaken, startled, with the sensation of an army of ants sucking at my veins. At times, I thought it was Dalila, but when I turned on the light I would find her wound up like a centipede, with a *Mimosa pudica's* mournful look about her. I would turn out the light and within moments have the same feeling: tiny tentacles sucking on my pores, coiling into my hair, kissing my belly. I would wake up shaking and soaked in sweat. I might have spent the whole night this way, awakening with a start every few minutes, if, on one of the occasions that I turned on the light to check on Dalila, I hadn't glanced over at my arm reaching toward the lamp and found little pink blotches, like bites. I leaped out of bed and found, to my horror, my face, neck and stomach also covered.

I looked back at Dalila, confused by her inertia and my condition. I pulled the bed away from the wall and was instantly left breathless at what I found living there. Dozens of tiny Dalilas had sprouted, and these had multiplied and spread all around the bed and the corners between the floor and the wall. At the sight of me, they stretched out their vines and scuttled—some toward the bed, others up the wall, toward Dalila, who lay petrified; and still others came toward me. At that moment I knew there was no escape.

Originally published in our Summer 2017 issue,
Kitchen Table Translation

Vão / Vòng: A Conversation with Katrina Dodson

Madhu Kaza

If someone had to inadvertently access my email inbox, I'm glad it was Katrina Dodson. I met Katrina in July 2016, while I was teaching Elizabeth Bishop and writing about Clarice Lispector. Katrina, an Elizabeth Bishop scholar, is an acclaimed translator of Lispector. Last July, we were both on a college campus in upstate New York. I forgot to log out of my Gmail account on a public computer, and when Katrina came across the emails in my inbox with subject lines such as "crônicas draft" and "Self-Portrait in Green" (Marie NDiaye's novel, which she knew and loved), she momentarily confused the account for her own. When she told me about it later, it seemed as though that accident was a serendipitous introduction. I was delighted by our shared affinities, and my admiration for her work. Our exchange emphasized the intersections between translation, personal history, and cultural difference.

MHK: Can you talk about the relationship between your sense of identity and your work as a writer and translator from Brazilian Portuguese?

KD: I've always felt at odds with mainstream American culture. and I think that has a lot to do with growing up in San Francisco and spending my formative years in majority non-white environments. both at home and at school, where a lot of my classmates had immigrant parents. My mother is from a rural village in north Vietnam and didn't come to the U.S. until 1975—she met my father in Saigon, where he was stationed as a Foreign Service officer in the late 1960s. She was able to bring part of her family over here after the war, so as a child I was surrounded by relatives speaking Vietnamese even though we spoke mostly English at home. I identify as Asian American, and "hapa" more specifically, the term that came from Hawaii and that's been adapted in California to identify people of part-Asian descent. I recently learned that in São Paulo, the word "mestiço" most commonly refers to mixed-race Asians, though people there usually assume I'm half Japanese, since Brazil has the largest population of Nisei Japanese.

This background has led me to seek out cultures and languages beyond the dominance of American English—there's something appealing to me about being an outsider by choice rather than by default. I've always wanted to write more about Vietnam and from a more overtly mixed-race perspective, but as a result of some fateful decisions and general momentum, I ended up going much further in my relationship to Brazil.

My Asian heritage gets obscured by my European name, Katrina Dodson, especially since my writing and translations have mainly been focused on Brazil. People often respond with curiosity when they meet me and can tell I'm part Asian, or at least, not white. They're usually pretty good at hiding their initial surprise, but then the question of my background eventually finds its way into the conversation. Sometimes people just assume I'm Brazilian, and so it adds another level of surprise when I say I have no family connection to Brazil and that I'm half

Vietnamese. I've thought about using my middle name, Kim, which my parents chose because it's both a Vietnamese and an American name (in Vietnamese, it means "metal" and can become "gold," "silver," or other metals depending on what compound word it forms). But then people assume that I'm half Korean, so it makes things more confusing. I've wondered if I should add my mother's maiden name, to be Katrina Nguyen Dodson, to add that visibility to my name, and because I'm proud of my Vietnamese heritage. I wonder what effect that would have on how people view my work.

MHK: In your description of how you are read, there's a sense that your name is curiously illegible to people when they first encounter you and requires some further translation.

I'm curious about how you began translating from Brazilian Portuguese? Have you ever translated or thought about translating from Vietnamese? Do you have projects that connect you to your Asian background?

KD: I came to Portuguese rather by accident—by deciding to move to Brazil with a boyfriend back in 2003. I'd studied Vietnamese in college and spent a semester at Vietnam National University in Hanoi, but it's such a difficult language and was more daunting to try to master. When I first began my doctorate in Comparative Literature, I thought I'd be able to specialize in Brazilian literature in a comparative context, while also still being able to do some work with Vietnam. But the nature of academic scholarship meant I had to choose, and I chose Brazil, which has taken me down this path to translating Brazilian literature. It causes me some anguish to have such a close relationship to Brazilian culture, to often be mistaken for a Brazilian, and to feel less comfortable in Vietnamese contexts. It's easier for me to integrate into Brazilian culture, in part because Brazil is diverse like the U.S., and mixed-race people are the majority there. Plus, I don't take it personally when I make language mistakes or am pointed out as a gringa in Brazil. Vietnamese culture is more exclusive, and mixed-race people are often not accepted as true Vietnamese. So it's more fraught for me when I try to make inroads into the language and culture—I'm much more sensitive to "failing" when I speak Vietnamese or when I don't know something. But I'm not done with Vietnam yet. I'd still like to go back and spend more time there and be able to really speak with confidence. I'd like to write about my mother's life one day. More recently, I've thought of translating some Vietnamese poetry with her. I got the idea from working with poet Brenda Hillman on new translations of the Brazilian poet Ana Cristina Cesar, which Hillman began translating with her mother, who is American but grew up in Brazil.

MHK: I think many writers and translators who are the children of immigrants would connect with the anxieties and sensitivities you describe. I certainly do. I enjoy translating from Spanish—a language to which I have no ancestral connection—much more than from Telugu, which is my native language, but not the primary language of my literacy. I have the same sense of failure—in my case a feeling of failing in my first language, failing my origins and culture. Because Telugu is so important to me, and the language already signals a kind of loss in my life, working with it is very fraught. Every attempt at translation from Telugu feels like a repetition of the difficult experience of immigration, whereas I feel quite free when working from Spanish.

I'd love to see what you might do with your mother working from Vietnamese. I have asked my mother to help me at times with translation, and early on I believed that relying on my family for help delegitimized me as a translator. *Kitchen Table Translation* [a series of events curated by Madhu Kaza, then featured in a collaboration with Aster(ix) in an issue of the same name] arose in part from my re-evaluation of this notion. It's been great to hear from other writers about how they work with family members. At our first *Kitchen Table Translation* event in New York in November 2016, Genya Turovskaya spoke about calling her mother from college to ask her about specific words in an Anna Akhmatova poem. And Zohra Saed talked about the back and forth process of working with her father to translate poems from Turkestani. It's not only that I no longer think of such processes as illegitimate, but I also think that working in these ways can expand our understanding of what it means to translate, the way that translation crosses from the literary sphere into life and back.

Given that Brazil and Vietnam are two places that you have a connection to in different ways, have you found any resonances between your experiences of Brazilian Portuguese and Vietnamese? Or if there are not specific resonances, do you access particular experiences or feelings when you leave English (even if you return to it when you actually translate)?

KD: I've thought a lot about how the Brazil-Vietnam connection is somewhat random, and yet I'm always noticing similarities in my experiences with both places. Both are tropical countries, much poorer than the U.S., where a lot of life happens on the streets, in an informal economy. Both nations have a history of hardship and violence that somehow combines with an ability to maintain a certain lightheartedness through suffering and to enjoy just sitting on a stool and watching the world go by, something that Americans don't seem to know how to do very well. I suppose that could be said of a lot of tropical countries.

One convergence that I find more striking is an echo between the languages. Having studied Vietnamese unexpectedly gave me an instinctive understanding of Portuguese spelling and pronunciation, elements that often perplex foreigners. Both Portuguese and Vietnamese have a lot of nasal sounds, and both languages strongly favor open syllables—you never end a word on a closed syllable in either language, even if you see a consonant. For example, "vão," which can mean "they go" or "empty space" in Portuguese, sounds just like "vòng," which means "round" or "circle" in Vietnamese. The phrase "đi vòng vòng," means to go walking or cruising around, so I like to think of "vão/vòng" as a place where the two languages I'm closest to intersect.

Imperialism makes for strange bedfellows, and it turns out that the romanized Vietnamese alphabet is derived from the Portuguese because the Portuguese missionaries who came to Vietnam from Macau and Goa in the early 1600s were the first to convert the language from Chinese script into Roman characters. The French Jesuit Alexandre de Rhodes is credited with romanizing Vietnamese, but his 1651 dictionary drew heavily on work done by the Portuguese. So even though there are virtually no Vietnamese in Brazil, there is this unexpected linguistic connection.

In translating Clarice Lispector, I thought about her relationship to Portuguese as the child of immigrants who spoke with an accent and who brought other languages into the home—Yiddish and Hebrew. Lispector clearly dominates the Portuguese language in her writing yet makes these deliberate distortions that I feel must have started from having that window onto other languages that comes with being part of a diasporic community. Having to speak some Vietnamese with my relatives and listening to my mother talk on the phone in Vietnamese for hours definitely gave me a more imaginative relationship to English and to the givens of language in general than I otherwise would have had.

MHK: I think that's something that's not acknowledged widely enough: how access to multiple languages can enhance your imaginative capacities in your primary language.

-

Editors' note: this interview has been condensed and edited for clarity. The entire original conversation is available to read online.

Originally published in our Spring 2016 issue, *Atravesando*

The Eternal Pursuit of the Whale's Song

Keya Mitra

My fiancé Simon, my mother, and I boarded Air Hawaii from the Houston Intercontinental Airport around seven in the morning to visit my dying father. My mother, who came from a traditional Indian family, had still refused to grant my father a divorce even though she hadn't spoken to him since he'd retired a decade earlier from his engineering firm and moved to Honolulu. His assistant Emily—his only companion—was the one who called to tell us that my father was on his way out. But, always the dutiful wife, my mother booked a flight immediately. When I questioned the decision, she just kept repeating herself to avoid further argument. This was her M.O. "He's my husband," she said. "My *husband.* My husband."

"Yes," I said. "And it's insane to pretend you have a relationship with him. Insane. *Insane.*"

On the plane my mother sat herself between Simon and me. Her phobia of being peripheral was worse than her fear of death.

Simon hated my mother but hated confrontation even more, so he promptly fell asleep. I pinched his arm. His head bobbed, and his eyes flickered open. Then he drooled on my hand.

"Wake up," I hissed. We'd been dating for six months, engaged for three, and lately he'd been driving me crazy with his constant state of robotic calm. Even when he was awake he seemed half-asleep. Lately sex between us seemed meticulously planned (Simon was a mathematician). The motion of our lovemaking was like a see-saw, a steady up and down motion with little variation other than the occasional change in positioning. Did he stay up nights figuring out the intricate calculus of orgasm?

My mother lifted the armrest between us. Boundaries aggravated her, and she dispensed of them whenever possible. "Have the two of you talked about babies?" she asked.

"No," I said wearily. "We're not even *married*."

She clasped her hands together. "Every day, Leela," she said. "I pray every day." Then: "My mother didn't marry until she was twenty-six. Your age. She thought she had plenty of time. But then—poof! Her eggs dried up and her life was over."

"There was no poof," I said. "She had you, and she lived until she was 75."

"Oh, there was a poof all right," she said. "She wanted six kids and ended up with one."

She tucked my bra strap under my shirt. I'd been raised to think that God was always just around the corner with his Polaroid, ready to snap the picture that would be put to the committee on Judgment Day. If your bra strap or underwear ever made an appearance, that was it for you.

The groggy morning light strained to fill the plane. It was soporific, engulfing us like a giant yawn. My mother's wedding ring glinted in the sunlight. I hadn't seen it in years. It had become part of the tangle of jewelry in a drawer that had come to resemble a junkyard.

"Why are you wearing that?" I asked. "Oh right. It's your wedding ring. Your *wedding ring*."

She closed her eyes with a melodramatic sigh. A few minutes later, a tortoise-necked man on my other side began talking to us.

"Are you two on vacation?" The man asked.

My mother missed no opportunity to flaunt her tragedies. Her eyes flickered open. "No," my mother said, "my husband is *dying*."

He murmured his apologies, paused, then said: "Your husband sure was lucky to have such a gorgeous wife." I rolled my eyes.

My mother bowed her head. She wore a white button down shirt and pants, a loose outfit that seemed a slap in the face to the gorgeous tautness of her body. For her, any display of sexuality had to be entirely accidental; when someone complimented her on her shirt, she'd notice a "button she'd missed." Sexual suggestiveness was like shoplifting; it seemed to thrill her, but when confronted she denied it had been intentional.

But, even though she was all too aware of her beauty—which the smitten described as "exceptional" and the envious, like me, "fucking unjust"—she wore her loveliness like a kid given a necklace of pure gold. She was uneasy possessing it even as she reveled in its value to the outside world.

She was a pharmacist, and I began working alongside her as a pharmacy technician two years ago, just after graduating from the University of Houston. She couldn't bear to be alone after my father moved, so I took the job to be near her. When I was a child, my mother told me that she had pursued pharmacy to help people heal and to carry on the legacy of her father, a doctor in Kolkata who'd treated many of his poorer customers for free. But she tended to be sympathetic to only the most "appropriate" conditions and illnesses. Influenza was acceptable; gonorrhea was absolutely not.

But my mother's loveliness duped others into deeming her a saint. One customer at the pharmacy referred to her as a "Hot Mother Teresa," especially once he heard that she was nursing an ailing husband. My father was diagnosed with Multiple Sclerosis in his twenties and by his early forties had been confined to a wheelchair. After he got sick, my father grew immune to my mother's charms and to the charms of the world around him. He stopped speaking unless absolutely necessary. Around him Mom constantly clamored to make noise, trying to make herself heard. Even after my father disappeared from our lives, she never lost the habit of seeking attention.

The next hour and a half consisted of my bearing witness to Mom's grotesque flirtation with Turtle Man. I tried to shake Simon awake; he rewarded me with more spittle. So I tapped my mother on the knee. "Switch seats with me." She didn't put up a fight; now that she had Turtle's attention, I was off the hook for a while.

Simon's hair was strewn carelessly over his eyes. The near perfection of his nose, combined with the sharpness of his cheekbones, created the illusion of arrogance. I'd fallen for him in part because of his name—I'd had a crush on Simon Le Bon from Duran Duran for years, and the fact that my Simon resembled the lead singer (aside from being Indian) seemed too much of a coincidence for me to ignore.

Comfortably seated next to Simon, I sang Duran Duran's "My Name is Rio" into his ear until he couldn't fake sleep any longer. "You win," he said after attempting to drool on me a few more times. He grabbed my hand, kissing it briefly. "But you better be carrying Xanax on you. You realize that the FDA approved it after meeting your mother."

My fingers slid into his. His hands were beautiful and soft.

I'd met Simon at the pharmacy several months earlier. My mother's eyes scanned his body when he walked in. He had all the prerequisites—Indian, with a good build, no evident piercings. As he slid a prescription to my mother, she glanced at it, wagged a finger at him, and said, "Yes! I knew I'd seen you before."

"I'm sorry," he said, shoving his hands into his pockets. "I don't think we've met—"

"Years ago," she insisted. "You used to build Lego castles with my daughter Leela. We spent some time with your family when the two of you were children."

I was filling an order at the time. "I don't remember ever building a Lego castle, Mom," I called out.

"You spent *hours* building Lego castles," she said. She stepped back, grabbed my sleeve, and guided me to the counter. "Leela here stole my bindis and put them all over her face and told you that she had a rare strand of Monster Pox. You were so scared of her, Simon. You ran around the house screaming *Monster Pox, Monster Pox.*"

According to my mother, I'd coincidentally had childhood friendships with several Indian males (always in their twenties) who'd walked into the pharmacy.

A new customer approached my mother, and I took the opportunity to whisper to Simon: "I'm sorry. She's totally lying. We never built Lego castles together. My mother scares me sometimes."

He laughed. "*Pharmacists* scare me."

"Why?"

"You have my life in that computer," he said. "A prescription can be as intimate as a diary. You could write a whole book about me if you wanted."

"Right," I said, "because you're *that* interesting." He grinned. And I began to feel an intense attraction to everything about this man I didn't know.

Two days later, he came in with a prescription for Cipro and a reservation at an Italian restaurant for the following night.

Our flight landed at 5:02 p.m. My mother called Emily on the cab ride to the hotel. The woman said that my father had died at approximately 4:32 p.m., which sounded like no approximation at all, and my mother hung up and stared at Simon and me like a bird that had just slammed into a glass window.

We were staying at the Royal Hawaiian, a pink palace overlooking Waikiki Beach. Though my father never spoke to us again after he left, he sent my mother checks without fail every month, so she was as rich as she was miserable. As we passed through the lobby, a man and woman were taking their vows, impeccably dressed and holding hands like figurines you'd see on a wedding cake. The view was beautiful, but the wedding seemed zoo-like. Strangers wearing sand-coated flip-flops and swimsuits stopped and gawked. Then they kept walking, talking loudly.

The room Simon and I were sharing had the pink sheen of the rest of the palace. It had a large balcony and windows, and the splashes and screeches and warmth outside flooded our room. I stretched out on the bed. In the fullness of the sunlight my stomach seemed more sensual in its softness. Everything was new. I pulled at Simon's pants, and he turned around.

I winked at him.

"Honey, your dad just died."

"I haven't seen him in ten years," I said. "There's no need for me to go celibate."

He sat beside me on the bed and gazed out the window. "But he was your father."

I'd told Simon about Dad—about how in his early twenties he'd been training to run in the Olympics when he was diagnosed with MS. After that, he self-medicated to tolerate the gradual wasting away of his body. But I hadn't told Simon about the last time I visited Kolkata with my parents, when I was eleven. I told him about the visit now, about how my father's pendulous stomach flattened within the first fourteen days of our visit, and the heaviness of his eyes diminished for some time. In his childhood Dad made his own fighter kites out of bamboo sticks and rice paper, and he laid them out for me on his childhood bed like a shy kindergartener. The colors were bold—purple, blue, red—and I could see the kites had been made in spurts of exhilaration, in the midst of a vision of himself as a creator, an innovator. The tissue was poorly pasted and torn. I pointed this out, and he said: "Well, I was only a boy when I made them," he said. I had never imagined my father as a boy. I had to close my eyes and picture him, a child, inhabiting this strange house years ago.

When he asked me if I wanted to fly the kites, I saw the child in my father once again—his joy, pure and unfiltered, shone in his eyes. That was what I'd loved about Simon too. The childlike glee in his eyes.

"The kites you see in America are mostly for decorative purposes," he told me during our first lesson on the roof. He'd limped as he climbed the stairs up to the roof, but, once seated, he sat tall in his chair. "But these kites are alive; they have a mind of their own. They're called fighter kites for a reason; the goal is to cut other people's strings until your kite is the only one remaining."

The roof of my grandparents' home was concrete and flat. My father handed me a reel wound with a thin, transparent string made out of ground glue and glass. When he first mentioned flying kites, I fantasized he would burst into song like the father in *Mary Poppins.*

There was no singing, but my father was almost giddy as he freed his kite into the air and showed me how to release mine. My kite was defiant, delinquent, darting around in all directions. My father, on the other hand, was a puppeteer on an inverted stage; the kite's motions corresponded perfectly with the movement of my father's hands. His kite swooped in and cut mine, swiftly, gracefully, before sailing on.

At the end of the lesson he commanded: "Now cut mine." His kite was suspended, paralyzed, in the sky—an open target. With its wings spread apart, it looked like a victim of sacrifice as I fumbled with my reel. It bobbed patiently in the air like a martyr, in acceptance of its approaching death. It took several attempts, but I finally managed to sever the string in choppy, amateur movements. And then I burst into tears. Dad blinked, startled. Then he wrapped me in an awkward embrace. "It's just part of it, Leela. One kite has to lose."

Simon nodded, listening. "But you didn't want to win."

"It was something he'd made, Simon. That he made as a boy. And it was lost to the sky."

Simon smoothed back my hair, pulling my face to his torso. The gentleness of his touch still moved me. "Maybe he was trying to teach you something about saying goodbye."

"Well, duh. But I didn't want to say goodbye," I said. My face was pressed against his shirt, and I heard the petulance in my voice.

"Of course you didn't, baby," Simon said softly. Then he stepped back. "I'm going to get some fishing equipment while it's still light out," he said with a faint smile, "but I'll be back."

"You're going to leave me alone with her?"

"How about this," he said, his smile strained. "I'll bring you back a nice long rod."

"You better," I said. "I haven't seen a rod in a while."

I watched from the balcony as Simon made his way down the beach, his shoulders hunched. As handsome as he was, his posture was terrible. I imagined him as a kid, small and ill at ease with his body, and some of my warmth for him returned.

In the beginning, our love had been dizzying. On our first date, he blurted out, "You have beautiful arms."

"That I've never heard before," I laughed. I had been wearing a red strapless dress and worried all evening that my breasts were sprawled over the table on exhibition for all to see.

"Oh yeah," he responded. "They make me think of trees—tall, happy trees with the branches hanging over the water. They're lovely. Powerful."

"That makes absolutely no sense, weirdo," I said, laughing. But, as nonsensical as it was, the compliment roused me—it introduced the possibility of something surprising and real.

Over the next few weeks we groped one another with the desperation of teenagers breaking curfews; defying the idea of the austere match our parents thought they'd made. We violated their ideals in our secret moments—sex in Memorial Park behind a scrawny cluster of trees barely separating us from the passing joggers, crude verbal exchanges during love-making. I still lived with my mother, and our sexual trysts seemed a delicious contradiction to her outdated values.

"I might be starting to love you, Indian Simon Le Bon," I whispered one night as we groped in the parking lot outside a Kroger's.

"Then marry me, Indian Natalie Portman," he murmured, his breath warm against my ear.

It struck me months later that we'd essentially committed to marrying avatars, not real people. But I figured, back then, that engagement would naturally lead to emotional intimacy. Of course, it didn't. We'd reveled in deceiving our parents for so long, but once we had their approval we were left with our unformed selves. And soon our relationship became one long conversational pause—with pressure to speak, though nothing remained to be said.

I grabbed a blanket and settled into a chair on the balcony. Surfers skated over the frothy waves below. Off in the distance three naked men played soccer, kicking the ball as their genitals jumped around like pom-poms. I squinted, wishing I'd brought my binoculars. It had been weeks since I'd seen genitals—from near or afar.

My mother opened the hotel room with the spare key—of course she'd insisted on taking it—and sat down on the balcony. "Where's Simon?"

"Down at the beach."

She looked vaguely alarmed. "Without you?" She peered at the Pom-Pom genital boys on the beach. "Are those boys naked?"

I held up a hand. "What did you find out about Dad?"

"Your father wanted his body cremated," she said. "No funeral. I'm going now to see him. He's been moved to the funeral home. Do you want to come?"

I nodded—I had to—though the idea of greeting his corpse nauseated me.

She wiped her eyes with the side of her hand. "Your father must have loved it here."

He would have loved it. The vast expanse of sand. The openness of the sky.

During the last few weeks of our visit to Kolkata, my uncles flew their kites with my father, and the volume of conversation rose as their kites approached one another, dodged, and then attacked. My cousins, who were watching, roared like sports commentators, lauding or dismissing the kites. "That kite has no balls!" One cousin heckled. "It doesn't deserve to be black. It should be wearing a pink, frilly dress."

Gradually the kites acquired personalities—my father's kite, Obi-Wan Kenobi from *Star Wars,* was the meditative type. My oldest uncle's kite, named Fonzie after the *Happy Days* character, was overconfident—a self-assured teenager challenging the older virtuoso. When my father severed my uncle's kite, it wasn't without some sadness that we watched Fonzie float out of sight. Sure he was brash and pompous—but he was young, and he'd made a valiant effort. My father initially bristled with irritation when my uncles heckled him, but eventually he softened, unable to contain his laughter. It broke free with startling force, and my mother gaped at him. *Did you just laugh?* She asked. *My God, the sky must be falling!*

But underneath her mocking tone resided a deep, intimate respect. She would sit next to me and gaze reverently at my father like he was a prophet. It was easy during those moments to see how it had been different once between them, and the faint breeze around us was light with optimism, a hopefulness that faded soon after we returned to Houston. Soon after that trip he was confined to a wheelchair.

My mother rose from her seat on the balcony, and I followed her outside. She clutched her purse with both hands, as though it was in danger of being swept away by the wind. I held her hand as we waited for a cab.

Inside the casket my father's body was small and doll-like, his face almost shriveled. He was dressed in a white shirt buttoned to the collar. His fingers were splayed, his hands flat on his chest. I wanted to put something in his hands to bridge the vast, lonely space between them.

A year after we got back from India, my father and I went to the park to fly kites. My father hadn't gotten used to his wheelchair, and his movements were jerky, frustrated. The kites moved groggily through the sky. "It's this damn heat," he grumbled, swatting at the air.

"But it was even hotter in India," I said timidly. He said nothing. His kite had become lodged in an oak tree. I stood up to retrieve it, but he put a hand on my wrist to restrain me and wheeled himself over to the tree. He tried to stand and yank on the string, but he fell back into the chair with a thud.

My parents argued in their bedroom for hours after we returned. When it quieted I found my mother in the kitchen, staring into a glass of water. "He used to make magic," she said. "He refuses to even try anymore. He'll barely even talk to me."

I was silent, the marble floor cold beneath my feet. The month before he left us, my father passed his days in bed, staring blankly at the ceiling. I brought him his meals upstairs, and every time I came close to his motionless body I was terrified of finding a stiff corpse. I watched his belly, silently praying for it to rise. It always did, but my relief was short-lived. I mentally prepared for his death daily. Was happiness like food? I wondered. Once deprived of it for too long, would Dad eventually die?

The morning he left us for good, he wheeled himself to my bed and hugged me. My feet were bare, and at that moment I badly wanted a pair of socks. I was exposed, unprotected, without them. "My precious girl," he said, his head heavy on my shoulder. "I wish I could stand it, the wasting away of my body, my spirit. I wish I was vulnerable enough to let you watch it happen." His voice was hoarse, and when he let go my shoulder was damp from his tears. "Because you are so dear to me."

I said nothing. He'd left, in spirit, long ago. I watched him wheel himself out of my room, slumped in his chair. Nothing remained to attach him to the world.

My mother wept at my side. Emily stood quietly in a corner. She had organized his life after he moved to Hawaii, enabling him to live in virtual isolation. She was the conduit between him and the outside world: getting his groceries, making his phone calls, emptying his bedpan. Her demeanor was stiff, unobtrusive, asexual—everything my father would have wanted from an employee.

I couldn't cry. My father had taught me to sever ties with him that day I cut his kite and watched it disappear into the sky. I could have mourned at a ceremony, dressed in somber grey tones. There I could slip in and out of sadness as though it was a rented suit. But there was no funeral here, no collective grieving. There was only a body as still in death as it had been in life.

After we'd visited India for the last time, my paternal grandparents passed away, and my father's childhood home was sold. He'd only brought with him two kites—one of which we'd abandoned in the tree. The afternoon my father left us, I raced to the park on my bike, praying that the kite was still intact, securely tethered to the tree. But all that remained was a scrap of pink tissue dangling from a branch.

My mother virtually charged into Emily, hugging her tightly. "We were so in love. Did he talk about me often?"

Emily threw a desperate glance in my direction. *Tell the truth,* I thought. *Please.*

Emily looked away. "He spoke of you so fondly."

In the cab on the way back to the hotel my mother was still wailing. "Did you hear that? We were in love. *Emily* said. Emily *said.*"

I sighed and took her hand in mine. "I made reservations for us all to go snorkeling tomorrow morning. It'll take our mind off all this."

She sniffed. "We came to mourn. Not take a vacation."

"Stay at the hotel then and mourn," I said. "But grieving isn't a full time job. I need a distraction."

She didn't respond, and I knew she would come. Since my father had left us, she'd grown terrified of being unseen for too long. Even mourning had to be a group-activity.

I returned to my hotel room alone. The sun still lingered in the sky—a dazzling orange, it appeared to rise from the sea like smoke. It was hard to imagine it was making its descent. The bustle below had quieted to a low rumble of voices. A man walked alone by the ocean, which surged and retreated from the banks in a self-assured rhythm. A steady accumulation of murmurs came from a party inside a giant red tent parked perilously close to the ocean. The red flap floundered in the wind whenever a new couple entered.

My relationship with Simon deteriorated soon after we became a real couple. Shortly after our engagement, we spent the night together, and Simon began talking dirty in Bengali. I didn't have a clue what he was saying. My parents had planned on teaching me Bengali, but each held the other responsible for teaching me the language. So I never learned. Simon continued his crude Bengali monologue, and finally I said: "I'm sorry. I can only talk dirty in English."

"You don't speak Bengali?"

"No," I said, breathing on his neck, "but I can be more crass and inventive in English than you could ever imagine."

"Well, that's even better," he said, grabbing me. But he was more distant that night, and I felt like a felon. The awkwardness between us never went away. When Simon's parents called and he lapsed into long conversations in Bengali, I'd sneak away to the backyard, away from his laughter and warm words.

I changed into my flip-flops and bathing suit, seized by a need to shake myself out of chronic weariness. I grabbed a flashlight and then went downstairs. The air near the beach was chilly, and my throat was dry as I slogged through the wet sand. I passed by the red tent, where country music was playing, and people sang along, breaking into claps and whistles every few minutes.

I turned around and walked toward the tent, driven by a sudden desire to make my presence known. I lifted the red flap and stepped inside, where a couple was swaying drunkenly, belting out something resembling "Yesterday" by The Beatles. Middle-aged couples were pressed together. Wine glasses dangled perilously from their fingers. Children ran through the tent and jumped around holding hands, all joy and motion and eagerness. I realized after a moment that I had stepped into a wedding reception. I leaned against a wall. In the midst of family, I was anonymous. I left unnoticed.

A single seagull sat on the beach, facing the ocean. The smoke of the sunset had cleared. Soon there would be nothing left to see.

I found Simon on an isolated patch a mile from the hotel. His fishing rod hung limply from his hand. He was smoking a cigarette, inhaling with deep reverence the tiny torch with a faint flame at its end. His veneration for it made me want to hold one myself, as though we were in vigil. The light disappeared into the chunk of ash.

"Fish aren't biting," he said.

"Maybe they've gotten savvy," I said.

"How was it?" He stepped toward me.

I shook my head.

He reached over to squeeze my hand. "Leela, I wish I knew what questions to ask you."

"No one knows what to say after someone dies."

"I'm not talking about just now. I mean always. I wish I knew how to know you. To speak your language."

"Me too," I whispered. I rested my cheek, briefly, against the broadness of his back. And, for a second, he was no longer the illusory Simon Le Bon. He put out the cigarette and got down on his hands and knees, collecting brown and white pebbles from the sand. He flung a pebble into the sea, then another. I expected them to skip gracefully against the water's surface, but each brushed the surface and then sank.

"Maybe it's not about asking the *right* questions," I said finally. A massive, unwieldy rock sat at my feet. I bent over and picked it up with some effort.

"What do you mean?" He asked.

I flung it into the water, underhanded. The water splashed, slapping us in the face as the rock landed with a disgruntled thump. We began to laugh. Then Simon collected his gear, and we walked back to the hotel, hand in hand. He held his fishing rod in his other hand, like a cane in the sand.

"I mean," I said, "that maybe the problem is that we've stopped asking questions at all. Because we're afraid to admit what we don't know."

We hadn't walked together, side by side, for so long that we collided often. "How did our bodies fit so well together during sex," I said, laughing, "when we can't stop bumping into each other?" And before he said anything I realized it—our bodies hadn't aligned properly during lovemaking since we'd started to know, actually know, one another.

"Well, maybe it's okay to have bumpy sex for a while."

"Maybe. What's the name of this shell?" I asked, shining my flashlight down on the sand.

He knelt down. "I really don't know."

We kept walking. "Is that the Big Dipper?" I asked, pointing into the distance.

"Leela, I have no fucking clue," he said, doing his best Simon Le Bon accent.

I smiled. "You know you're actually nothing like Simon Le Bon," I said.

"Oh, I know it. And you are definitely no Natalie Portman."

We couldn't stop laughing. I could keep making Simon up, filling in the gaps through the prescriptions I'd filled for him. That was what my parents had done after all—lapsed into silence. Stopped asking the uncomfortable questions. Or we could revel in all that was unknown, mysterious to both of us. And find a way to create our own language.

When we arrived back at our hotel room Simon fell asleep, his arm slung over my chest. His body was warm, substantial. Real. So many nights I had stayed up, trying to match my breathing to his. But I could never quite keep pace with his quick inhalations. That night, for the first time in many months, I let myself breathe naturally. And I slept deeply, and well.

My mother fetched us before dawn, and we dragged ourselves downstairs to a van labeled "Dolphin Expedition." As we crawled into the back seat, the other passengers, a couple and their child, sang their hellos.

"You here on vacation?" The man asked. He wore a Hawaiian shirt unbuttoned to midway down his chest. His wife wore a tight pink halter top and obscenely bright orange lipstick. The boy swayed back and forth with impatience.

"No," my mother spoke up. "My husband died. We were very much in love—"

"That sucks," the wife said, cutting her off. My mother sat back, visibly annoyed, and I covered a smile with my hand. I wrapped my arm around her shoulder.

The woman went on: "Last night, we were just trying to play our guitar by the hotel pool, and these people *complained*. Such *prudes*."

"Yeah," her son repeated. "Total prudes."

When we arrived, we were guided to a boat, and we sat on the sides as it whirred through the water. The breeze was cool on our faces, and when I looked at Simon he was smiling. We both were. The Prudes' son refused to take off his cowboy hat, and he waved his arms over the side of the boat, chanting "DolphinsDolphinsDolphinsDolphinsDolphins" until the hat was swept into the water, and he broke into tears. After a while the boat paused in the water, and the instructors helped us put on our goggles and gear.

"Will the dolphins come to us?" My mom asked, worry straining her face.

"Dolphins are very warm and friendly," the instructor said. "They love people. They get excited whenever they see humans, and they show it by spinning."

The instructor dropped a microphone into the water, and a deep, elephant-like moan vibrated through the water. "That's the song of a humpback whale," she said. "Every mating season, a new male creates a unique song, and the rest of the whales echo it. You can hear it from miles away. It always sounds closer than it actually is."

"It sounds like Chewbacca from *Star Wars*," The Prudes' son said.

"Time to get in the water," the instructor said.

We dangled our legs over the side of the boat as the instructors nudged us into the water, one by one. As the instructor prodded the Prudes into the ocean, I felt sick, as though we were all being forced into a mass grave. The bodies toppled over and splashed in the water.

"We'll meet back here," Simon whispered, standing behind me. Then it was my turn, and after the initial shock the water was surprisingly warm. The snorkeling mask was tight on my face, and I tugged on it. "Heads down," the instructor shouted from the boat. "You'll miss the dolphins if you keep looking up. Stay underwater."

Legs flailed underwater, indistinct as strands of seaweed. My mom was behind me, pulling at my ankles. She said: "You can't leave me alone."

"You need to look for them yourself," I said, squeezing her arm. "You'll survive without me."

I pulled the mask over my face and dipped my head underwater, moving my legs like scissors to propel myself forward. My breath emerged in short gasps. When I came up from underneath the surface, Simon bobbed in the distance. Or at least I thought it was him. I couldn't pick him out definitively from the rest of the bodies encased in life vests. I waved in his general direction, then swam on.

The song of a whale vibrated through the water, a deep, definitive sound, and I felt a sudden chill. I ducked my head back under the surface with my eyes wide open, while the mournful wail shook the waters. I wanted, more than anything, to be engulfed in the haunting music.

The whale could have been miles away, I knew, but I thrashed toward the source of that howl. The ocean trembled, and then, just as suddenly, the rumble was gone. The others were even farther away, and I realized I'd been swimming in the other direction from them for some time.

I ducked below the surface again, and below me a school of six dolphins swam like a mirage before the ocean swallowed them up. I followed them, my arms making wide arcs. But they'd soon disappeared. In the distance, I heard the Prudes yelp with delight as the dolphins sprang up around them, spinning up in the air.

Around me the ocean was vast and thick and unknowable. I wondered if the dolphins gravitated toward all humans, or whether they approached only those who were fully alive. I imagined my father bobbing in the water with a lifejacket, waiting for the dolphins to come. Perhaps they'd sense he had left most of himself behind in that childhood home in Kolkata filled with handmade kites, and they'd swim past him, dismissing him as a corpse.

The others climbed back into the boat, ending their courtship of the dolphins. My mother and Simon waved, gesturing at me to swim back. I waved in return. I would rejoin them soon. But for now I paddled further away and waited, hoping that the whale would continue singing its raw, haunting song, and the dolphins would spin above the water in a magnificent display of camaraderie, pronouncing in their emphatic dance: *You are not yet dead.*

Appeared online in April 2014 at asterixjournal.com

Summer of Nene

Ivelisse Rodriguez

I was there when he fell. We were fucking around in Central Park. Had been smacking bitches on their asses and then had been running away from them. Then one started yelling real loud and this cop appeared out of nowhere and we just started running. Nene was behind me, he was always smaller, more frail—that cat was always sick, ever since he was a little kid, there was always some shit wrong with him. So I'm just jettin but I always used to look over my shoulder for him. That was a habit. But this time I heard him scream before I looked, and then I see my man go down over some rocks. And he tumbles and I imagine that the rocks pierce his back and he's stuck there for life. Me and the cop get to him at the same time, and my instinct is just to grab him. But this cop dude is like no, you should leave him where he is, that I'll hurt him more. But everything in me is fighting to grab him and pull him up. He looks all fucked up, like someone dropped Humpty Dumpty, and I want to put him back together. Set everything right, so he's whole again. Nene was always strong, I mean he was always sick but you know he was always down to go outside with us and terrorize the neighborhood. And he would play with that sick shit too. See everyone on the block knew that he was the sick one and no matter what he had done the previous day, they always let the shit go. So sometimes I would have to leave him where he was because I knew that he wasn't going to catch it but my ass would if I stayed long enough.

* * *

It didn't even start with his sucking my dick. No foreplay shit like that. I read books, watch movies and it always starts like that, the inevitable creep to the dick. Nene was sleeping over my house and my house was finally quiet at three in the morning and that's when he starts. I have my back to him with nothing but my underwear on. And then I feel it next to me, on my skin. Right up against my ass. Then he's pushing harder, trying to find the hole and then he breaks through and it's a whole new life.

* * *

The next morning he looks sick as shit, coughing all over the place, so my moms takes him home because she's scared I'll catch whatever he has. But she doesn't understand that never have I caught what Nene has. But she becomes the concerned mother all of a sudden and she takes him away.

* * *

After the fall, we are all sitting in the hospital waiting. And I cry, but not those tears of sadness, it's the tears of anger. The kind where you can't breath, my face gets all hot and I can't hold it in anymore. Guttural noises are scattered in with my language. My fists are in a ball and I just want to hit myself. My mother doesn't understand this rage, but if only she would just shut the fuck up and let me cry…all she's done is tell me that I have to be strong and not cry. But what does strength have to do with love?

He doesn't get out of the hospital for weeks and when he does, he can't walk anymore. I'm on the stoop and we see him coming down the street, but Nene doesn't look all sad and shit. For us nothing has changed, so we're just happy to have him home. His mother won't let him come out today, though. She says he has to rest in his bed first, figure out how to go to the bathroom and shit like that. That makes him sad. But then he knows he'll be out tomorrow. I come out the next day and I wait for him. It's me and Kenny that are just waiting and by like 11 he's still not down there. So I stand on the sidewalk and I yell, Neeeneeee, Neeeneeee, over and over again until his moms sticks her head out the window and starts yelling at me. Don't I know he can't walk? So I need to get my lazy ass upstairs and knock on the door like a normal human being. I laugh and I run up because at least I know he can come out and hang with us. He's still sitting in his bed when I get there. The lock of hair on his forehead is wet. And I'm like my man you need a haircut, you look like John Travolta and shit. His house is mad hot. I pull the covers off of him and his legs look like my sisters, thin and pale. Not me. I'm already brown but this burning summer has me even darker, so if I was sick you wouldn't be able to tell just by looking at me. You can see everything written on this cat's face. On his body. I pick him up and I put him in his chair. Then I wheel him to the bathroom. But I make the ride exciting, I'm crashing into the wall, I try to zoom here and there, but in reality his apartment is too small for that. I call his mother to shower him. I'd be scared to undress him, to see him naked. I always have my back to him and it's always unexpected. I expect it whenever he's in my house, but I can't tell you the precise moment, only that it is after the house is quiet. I tell her I'll be downstairs waiting for him. She's like you better not fuck around, I need you to come back up here because I need you to carry Nene down the stairs.

* * *

I go downstairs and have all this energy, but all I can do is wait for Nene. Kenny sits on the stoop but I'm on the sidewalk, walking from here to there, the length of the stairs, and I'm telling him a story real loud. Then Jessica, this girl in my eighth-grade class walks by, and Jessica has the fattest ass. And she's like, Hey Jimmy, what's up? Then Kenny perks up. She stands in front of me and the way she moves from side to side, I know she's showing off for me. And I look at her and smile. I give her that *papi* smile. And in that instant, I've moved from boy to man. I think of this bitch under me. I know who I'm supposed to be. With Nene though, I know who I am. She starts laughing at whatever shit I tell her and she glitters in the sun. In mid-laugh, hers, Nene appears. His stepfather has brought him down and barks at me to get his wheelchair. He leaves Nene at the bottom of the stoop and I run upstairs. When I get back downstairs, I've forgotten all about Jessica.

* * *

I never realized how important words are until I see them fight. I watch them to see what it's like to be in a real grown up relationship. They spend all their time in front of the T.V. now. No giggles coming from her bedroom. No desire to be alone, alone with their love. When I come in, I sit in the living room with them because if they are going to fight, they'll do it with me in the living room. It won't matter. They won't notice that I'm there. What they have to say to each other is much more important than my being there. I have never seen so much of my mother before this summer, so much of her emotions. Sure, she's fought with her other boyfriends before this, but I have never paid so much attention before. It held no interest for me. In the middle of their fighting, I look at the picture of them next to the T.V. They are at a picnic and he's hugging her from behind. The way they fight though it's like the fights they have on T.V. It's like they don't have their own words. She says things like: How can you do this to me and don't you love me anymore? Her words may not be real but I know that her pain is. Even if her reaction is straight out of a soap opera.

I can see the arteries in her heart choking her. The way that she can barely breathe and the tears stream down her face. Cutting off her breath.

It almost breaks my heart.

He says things too that I have heard before: You make me do this. You're overreacting. I don't know what you're talking about.

I know what they are going to say that I can almost mouth along and anticipate what their next words will be. And it seems like the same fight every few days. This time though she turns and punches the wall and leaves. And he does nothing that I don't expect him to do; he doesn't cry, he doesn't sit in a chair and try to talk to me about this. Nothing. He does what he is supposed to do. He yells some curses at the slammed door. And he leaves a few minutes later saying how he doesn't need this shit. Then there is silence.

* * *

In the middle of the summer Kenny's mother goes to PR and the first night that she is gone he invites us over, me and Nene and some of the other fellas from the block. He also invites some girls over. As soon as the girls get there I start to get nervous. We sit on the living room floor and we start to play spin the bottle. But the girl gets to decide where she is going to kiss the guy. Jessica spins first and she gets Kenny and she kisses him on the cheek. Rebecca spins next and she gets Nene; she giggles nervously, stands up and kisses him on the cheek. But when Jessica spins again she gets me and she takes me into Kenny's moms room and just keeps kissing and kissing me on the mouth. We both come out smiling because everyone is looking at us. I look at Nene but he looks beyond us.

As soon as the girls leave, Kenny turns to me and asks me what happened with Jessica.

"Naw, nothing really happened. It was no big deal."

"Yeah, tell us what happened," Nene chimes in before he turns around and goes down the hall to the bathroom.

"No big deal? Is that why you had that kool-aid smile on your face? Come on man, tell us what happened. Did you touch her titties? Anything?"

"Naw, she was talking at first waiting for me to kiss her then she must've got tired of waiting and kissed me. She's cute, but you know, I'm not really feeling her."

"Nigga, are you gay? What's not to like? That bitch is fine."

By the time that Nene returns, Kenny has moved on and is telling me about him and Rebecca.

* * *

We never speak about what we do. Our words come in the form of knots in our hearts, glances, and brief touches on the hot of my back.

After the girls go home, we all go into Kenny's room to sleep. He has two twin beds and Nene and I crawl into one. I know he won't touch me tonight because Kenny is here. But I can't sleep. He's so close to me. And I don't know if he will understand about Jessica. That there is no desire there. It's not so much mechanical, but I love the fact that I can kiss her in front of so many people. The flaunting of it. And when I let her kiss me, I think of Nene, and I wish that she was him. That he could sit across from me, spin bottles and that we could kiss in front of a 2, 3, 6 people. He's asleep and his breath is against my neck and it warms my entire body. I push against him, so I can feel the part of his lips on my back. And maybe this is as public as we can get.

* * *

It has to be the hottest day that we have had all summer long. But of course we say that every day. The little girls across the street have been sucking on icees and limbés all morning. They've been running back and forth to the bodega since they have been out here. Kenny and I are too hot to even talk. We've been waiting for Nene to come down for like at least half an hour but in this heat it seems like 2 hours. I lay back on the step and look up at the sun and wonder how the fuck it can get so hot. When Nene gets downstairs, he's pale as shit and I'm like how come this dude doesn't get any darker in the summer. It's hot out here.

"Damn, I just found out I have to go to Wilson High School next year," Nene says when his stepfather leaves.

We're sitting on his stoop in the middle of the summer and this comes as a blow because for the past few days we had been making plans about how we were going to take care of Nene during the school year. How we were going to take turns picking him up in the morning and walking with him, carrying his books and shit like that.

"Why?" Kenny and I ask.

"Richmond High says they can't accommodate students in wheelchairs," Nene responds. "This shit sucks man, can't do shit because of this fucking wheelchair. Everything is getting all fucked up."

Kenny and I don't say anything to that. We see that Nene is about to cry. This is the only time that we have seen him get upset about the wheelchair. I can't imagine a time that we haven't all been in school together.

"Damn, and that's a tech school, what are you going to do there?" Kenny asks.

"I don't know man. I don't think I even know someone that goes to school there," Nene says.

"Yeah, me either," Kenny says.

We sit in silence and behind my sunglasses, I watch Nene. Because of the heat, Nene is sweating a lot. The back of his legs stick to the cloth of his seat. The heat makes it unbearable to just be in my shorts, so I can imagine how miserable he must be now.

"Man, it's too hot to be out here, I'm going back upstairs. Jimmy, take me upstairs. I'll see you guys later," Nene says.

"Naw, man, don't go. We can go to my house and chill in the AC or we can go somewhere," I say.

"No, I'm just going to get back in bed," Nene says. "I'll find you guys later."

Kenny and I eventually make it over to his moms house. He turns on the AC, even though his mother will kill him if the bill is too high when she gets back. We lay under the AC and start watching T.V. Kenny turns to me and asks me what's been on my mind ever since I've known Nene.

"I don't know, Kenny," I say, for once allowing myself to take the question seriously. "He's always been sick. You weren't there the day he transferred into our third grade class. He fainted that first day but then he came in the next day and punched this kid in the face that had laughed at him for fainting. He's a tough little fucker, but I don't know man. This summer has been worse than usual but that's probably just because of the accident."

When I had taken him upstairs, he had his arms around my neck and for the first time ever he kissed me, and it's the same way with the sex, he rushes in, no soft kisses, but insistent and throbbing. And when he pulls away, because it's always him pulling away, I feel sapped and like my world isn't the same; it's depleted. He takes my strength from me, but it's just to take, because he never gets stronger.

* * *

She stands above me and dares me to kiss her. Kenny leans against a car in front of us and smirks at me. She's wearing a tank top and I can see that she's not wearing a bra. She has long legs that are covered with tiny black shorts. She is pretty, and I can see how pretty she will be in years to come. I lean back and I lick my lips. I tell her to come here and when she leans in I kiss her. I taste every corner of her mouth and I think about T.V. and how people fall in love, have families and spend lives together. Not like it is around here, though people do fall in love, at least for a little while. My mother's last boyfriend was around for a year but before that she had had boyfriends here and there. And I wonder what makes love last.

* * *

I have spent all week waiting for his mother to leave. Nene's mother and stepfather were going away to the Dominican Republic for a week, so she asked me if I could stay with Nene for the week. I got my moms to agree real quick. I've been imagining that we can act like a married couple. We can watch videos in the bed. We can eat cereal when we want or just whatever we want. Nene's mother said she was going to leave me money and food in the refrigerator for us. I take a shower before I get there and try to look a little nicer than I have all summer. I knock on the door and my heart is beating real fast. I thought about buying him flowers or something but I didn't know how that would look or how he would feel about that. So I just show up empty-handed. He opens the door and I smile at him like I smile at Jessica. He looks unhappy and he turns and goes into the living room.

"Hey, what's wrong man?" I ask.

"Nothing, man."

"Oh."

I turn to look at him and I see that his hair is flopping down on his forehead. I reach out to smooth it away from his forehead so he won't be hot and he glares at me. I take my hand away and think about what it is that could be bugging him. I'm thinking that maybe Kenny told him about Jessica.

"Yo, man, aren't you excited that we are going to spend the whole week together?" I ask.

I don't know if I should proceed because we have never talked about what goes on between us. But I feel like I will burst if I sit here and don't say anything. I've been waiting all week to be alone with him, just so we can have this one week, even if it's the only week that we'll ever have together. So I gather the courage. I walk over to his chair and I pick him up. He doesn't say anything. I walk to his room in silence and I lay him on his bed. Now he just looks at me. I take off his shirt and kiss him on his neck. I pull down his shorts and rub my hands over his legs. I work my way up and down with my tongue. I finally put him in my mouth and he quivers and quivers under me, until he can't move anymore.

* * *

In the middle of the night he wakes me up and asks me if it's true, if it's true about Jessica.

"What's true?" I mumble.

"I've seen her looking for you. She's always asking Kenny where you're at."

"You know she likes me. Especially, from Kenny's party. I don't like her. I kissed her another time other than that but that's only because Kenny was there. I don't like her at all."

"So why kiss her at all?"

I explain that she comes looking for me. Usually I can keep from doing anything with her, but sometimes she persists and Kenny is there so I feel that I have to kiss her.

He lies on his back and whispers, "That's not a really good reason. You kiss her because you like her or you don't kiss her because you don't like her."

I stay silent. Our silence and the air conditioner are the only sounds that hang between us. I know he's right and I know he's wrong. I think about the inevitable, that this summer will come to an end, that in next year's school hallways there will be no Nene there and Jessica will surround me at every turn. I look at him as he sleeps and at least I know that this will never deteriorate like my mother's relationships, that we'll only be left with the pretty hum of this love and the last thing that we won't remember is the slamming of doors.

* * *

The next day when I bring Nene outside to meet Kenny, he's quivering in my arms, almost like a fish out of water. And I feel the sun melding us together as we stick to each other. And all I can do is look at him in public, this one time, no back to his, his breath on the front of my neck this time. I'll never have the words. And I think that's better–I think they could destroy, never tell what's in the heart, something close, so close but they could trap the wrong sentiment, the wrong *what* I was trying to get at and Nene would get stuck there. So I look at him and he stops moving and both our hot hearts are sticking to the hot concrete.

A radio turns on on the first floor, Kenny starts to talk about what we should do, the gypsy cabs start honking, a lady is yelling at her man. The world wakes up.

10th Anniversary Issue

Author Comments

Ivelisse Rodriguez on "Summer of Nene"

Reflect on the piece and your journey with it.

"Oh, 'Summer of Nene' is my favorite story in your whole collection," I would often hear. This would make me mutter with resentment under my breath. There were plenty of other stories that I despaired over, stared into the abyss over, and fought for every word that would never win the coveted "favorite" spot. What did this say about my writing if people loved more a story that I barely wrote? This isn't a confession of plagiarism; rather, it's a confession that writing, very rarely, is as woo-woo as you might think. In two different years, in two different cities, I sat down to free write and came up with the first half and the second half of this story in a matter of hours. I fiddled with the last few lines, but that's all the real revision I did. Very rarely will something come out so fully formed. And fully formed it was. "Summer of Nene" was my first publication; it garnered me a finalist distinction to a fellowship, which led to my agent many, many, years later; and it's been republished in English and Portuguese. And here again, in 2023, it resurges in this anthology.

The way I think of "Summer of Nene" now is as a gift from the muse, universe, ancestors, or anything/one else in the gift-giving business. This was a gift that was a doorstop, allowing my foot to cross over from unpublished to published, an incarnation of Elegguá, abriendo puertas. This story was not a fight because I had already fought so much to write and to be a writer, and the story partly came from all that stored goodwill. And maybe this "Elegguá story"--one that sets us off on our journey, pushes us forward to a future that is a labyrinth of open doors—is another way for the universe to whisper, "You're ready."

Appeared in our Fall 2017 issue, *Dirty Laundry*
Featured in *Best Small Fictions 2018 @BraddockAveBook*

House Call

Melissa Lozada-Oliva

katharine is getting her monthly brazilian wax **$$** she isn't seeing anyone **$$** so this isn't for anyone **$$** you shouldn't do anything unless it's for yourself **$$** katharine is a self-made kind of woman **$$** mami is too **$$** katharine comes to the house & mami waxes her in the living room **$$** she makes me set up the dining room table into a waxing bed **$$** the same one we eat our twisted thanksgiving on **$$** arroz con gandules even tho we aren't puerto rican **$$** sweet potato casserole recipe mami got from one of her clients **$$** katharine comes on time **$$** she has no tolerance for people being late **$$** i am reading in the kitchen but eavesdropping **$$** immigrant kids know how to listen **$$** it is how we get ahead **$$** we are good little spies **$$** katharine says have you heard about this george zimmerman thing? **$$** mami says no, what is about? **$$** katharine says well everyone wants to make it a race thing but it isn't a race thing because george zimmerman is latino **$$** mami says okay lift up your legs **$$** mami says to be honest, i don't really get it **$$** katharine says i just don't know why people have to be politically correct about it **$$** later, katharine will play devil's advocate with morals on facebook, later still, she will say we are all immigrants, aren't we **$$** now she says i mean you came here & worked so hard i just really admire that **$$** mami calls my name **$$** meleessa please heat up de wax **$$** oh, katharine says, your daughter, i haven't seen her in ages **$$** is she still reading? she is so well-behaved **$$** you did such a good job with them **$$** you always do such a good job

Originally published in our Fall 2013 Issue, *The Fiction Issue*

Earth-Language

Katie Gutierrez

Somehow, a wild animal—a tacuache or bobcat, some thrashing taloned thing—had gotten trapped in Maria Vega's belly; it tussled and clawed, ripping at her velveteen insides. She could do nothing as her bowels released. The smell, sharp and ripe, woke her younger brother, Guillermo, with whom she shared the twin-sized bed.

"What is *that*?" he asked, moving away from her in the darkness.

Maria rolled onto her side and hugged her knees to her chest. She pinched and twisted the sensitive flesh inside each arm to distract herself from the pain. When she opened her mouth, a sound like a chicken squawk emerged.

"Maria? Are you okay?"

Agile and quiet, Guillermo eased from bed and grabbed the flashlight they used when they needed the outhouse. Maria turned away from the light, but she heard Guillermo's disgusted gasp.

"Don't tell Abuela," Maria said, shivering. "I'll wash the sheets."

"Don't be stupid." Guillermo was already directing the flashlight toward the bedroom door. He maneuvered around the mattress on the floor where their six-year-old twin brothers were still sleeping. "You're sick and she's a curandera. She'll know what to do."

For the next few hours, Maria felt her body ripple in the shimmering waves that rose from the pavement in the summertime. She couldn't tell if her eyes were open or closed, if she was crying out or in. The only things grounding her to this world were the hands running a soaked sponge over her body, and she would later remember the awful moment of prescience just before being sick again, when time collapsed and there was not a second to warn her abuela, who calmly lifted her from the washbasin, drained the soiled water, replaced her in the basin, and ran the sponge over her again. Finally, when the animal had exhausted itself inside Maria, her abuela carried her to bed.

Abuela's bed was also twin-sized, pressed against the wall, always with the colorful quilt she'd made as a girl folded and tucked neatly at the end, like a bright sock at the end of a thin white leg. Maria's head reverberated with pain as Abuela murmured the Apostle's Creed. The soft words Maria heard every Sunday at Mass banged hollowly in her ears. Then something cool and smooth rolled over her face and chest, followed by each arm. It was an egg. It traveled from fingers to shoulder, shoulder to collar; from collar to shoulder, shoulder to fingers. Then a downward path from her forehead to her belly. Back again. An egg making a cross of Maria's body, her abuela praying in a fervent whisper. Gray hair, usually in a tidy bun, hung loose around her high-cheekboned face. Gently, she helped Maria turn onto her stomach. She rubbed the egg over Maria's bare back and down each leg to the soles of her feet. The few times Maria opened her eyes, she could make out the shapes of Guillermo and the twins over her abuela's shoulder. They paced the narrow hallway, paused at the doorway to the room, whispered, moved on. She fell asleep.

The next day, the weight of Maria's head no longer felt unbearable. She woke to her abuela perched lightly on the bedside, hair pinned back. Her penny-colored eyes were calm and alert, and her fingers lightly scratched Maria's scalp.

"Good morning, mijita. You're feeling better?"

Maria swallowed, wiggled her dry cow-tongue in her mouth. "I think so."

"Your fever is not so high anymore. Would you like to see the egg?"

The two sentences were strange, pressed up against each other. Maria nodded and groaned, pulling herself into a sitting position. "What happened to me?"

Her abuela reached for a glass that sat on the nightstand, filled with cloudy, grayish liquid through which Maria could make out the startling, sunflower-brightness of an egg yolk.

"Somebody gave you ojo," her abuela said.

"Ojo?" Maria repeated, stabbed aware and almost excited. Everyone knew what ojo was. Maria's friend Dianita had gotten it once. She stayed home from school for a week and came back hollow-eyed, her black hair lank and dry. She blamed it on the girl who sat behind them, who always complimented Dianita's glossy curls but never touched them.

"Si," her abuela said. "Look at how orange it is—no debe de ser ese color. And mira, look at the yoke. Do you see the shape of an eye?"

Maria took the glass and brought it closer to her face. At first it just looked like regular yolk disintegrating in dirty water, slimy white tendrils quivering. But the more she gazed, squinting, the more unusually bright the yoke seemed, like the sun spearing through morning haze. Almost cross-eyed now, she thought she could make out the crescent shape of an eye etched in the yolk's surface.

"What does it mean?" Maria asked. "Why would somebody want to give me ojo?"

"Probably they didn't mean to, but energy is powerful, and too much admiration is not so different from envy." Maria's abuela patted her shoulder. "Es temprano. Go back to sleep. I'm going to bury this in the yard."

Maria didn't hesitate. "I want to come."

After a beat, her abuela smiled. "Bueno, pues. Get your chanclas and put this on." She undid the snap buttons on her flannel bata, slipped off the housedress, and draped it around Maria. She stood barefoot in a thick-strapped ivory slip revealing the shape of her breasts and the line of her underwear where her skin folded over. Maria, unable to imagine her abuela going outside that way, tugged the end of the quilt from beneath the mattress and handed it to her.

They went to the backyard: Maria, her abuela, and the egg. The sparse yellow grass was wet with dew. The air smelled like the first bite of watermelon, juicy and crisp. Maria's stomach was still cramping, pulling in and twisting itself, but she didn't tell her abuela; she simply pinched the skin between her thumb and pointer until it hurt more than her stomach.

Beneath a techito, Maria's abuelo had built years ago, sat his old toolbox. Rust flecked from the lip as Maria's abuela pulled out a garden trowel. "Against the fence," she said, and Maria slowed her pace to match her abuela's as they tromped barefoot over the grass.

"Why are we burying it?" Maria asked.

"Eggs are the source of birth and life—they are how we all started in this world—and in their raw form, they are able to absorb the bad energies. Entonces we're not burying the egg; we're burying the bad energy. ¿Me entiendes?"

Maria frowned, coiling her fingers around the cool chain link fencing. "I think so. But will the neighbors get ojo, since we're burying the bad energy so close?"

"No. Once it's buried, it's gone."

The early morning sun slowly illuminated Maria's abuela as she finished digging and then poured the egg yolk from the glass into its grave. She tossed dirt over it and smoothed it with the trowel. When she was done, she slapped the trowel against the fence. Wet soil fell.

"Now let's thank Diosito for helping us heal you." Maria's abuela held out her hand, and Maria slid hers against it. Her abuela's fingers were plump and warm and familiar as they drew Maria's between them. "Padre nuestro, que esta en el cielo . . ."

Maria joined in the Our Father, but her gaze was on a tree in the neighbor's yard. Surrounded by overturned children's toys, the oak was young but tall, with slim graceful branches that reached languidly upward. In the spring breeze, the branches swayed in groups of three, four, five. It looked to Maria as if they were in conversation, women leaning toward one another, touching a shoulder or an elbow, confiding, confessing, and then, in big gusts of wind, bending at the waist to laugh until the breath in them was gone. Maria could hear that laugh in the rustle of leaves but didn't understand the joke making the slim branches wave frenetically back and forth. She was on the fringes of their conversation, and she was focusing so deeply on it that she didn't realize she had stopped praying.

"What do you see?" her abuela asked, watching Maria's face. "What are you hearing?"

"I don't know." Maria pulled her hand from her abuela's and again wrapped her fingers around the fence. She listened. "Something . . . something is different with the tree."

"Do you understand what the tree is saying?"

"No. Almost." Maria's body felt more alive, more receptive, than it ever had, as though the world was on the verge of revealing itself to her. "Do *you* understand?"

"Diosito speaks through the earth, and I listen. Sometimes I hear Him right. Sometimes I don't."

"How do you know when you hear Him right and when you hear Him wrong?"

Maria's abuela looked down at the trowel. She ran a finger through the dirt that remained, then rubbed that finger against her thumb. "Only He knows," she said. "But when the people get better, I think I heard Him right. When they do not, I accept that I did not understand His language."

"I want to know how to do it." Maria finally looked away from the tree, to her abuela. The pain in her stomach had calmed. "I want to know how to do what you do."

Maria's abuela tightened the bata that Maria had let fall loose over her shoulders. "I was your age when Diosito gave me the gift," she said softly. "Ven. Let's go inside. We will see with time if the gift develops. If it does, I will teach you to be a curandera."

* * *

Quickly, Maria became her abuela's apprentice. She left school in eighth grade, the year of the egg, and accompanied her grandmother all over south Laredo and into Nuevo Laredo. They walked the cobblestone square, Maria's abuela tracing a cross on the foreheads of children who scurried up to them, selling chicle and roses. (Maria thought they would have probably preferred pesos.) They visited the homes of people who had been given ojo or suffered from susto or who withered from illnesses that resisted every remedy the relatives knew to try. Maria watched her abuela soothe and cure sick infants, explain which yerbas to buy, how to pack them into little baggies and across which intersections to toss them. She marveled at how her abuela divined where in people's homes and yards hexed photographs or dolls were hidden and listened to her pray over strangers with the same intimate ferocity as she had when Maria was sick. Her abuela believed that she was speaking directly with Diosito and that He was listening; and the conviction, Maria recognized, made it true.

From the day she started her apprenticeship, Maria awoke at five-thirty a.m. The early hour was special—a lush, secret part of the day before the world uttered its last luxurious yawn and concealed itself again. Without waking Guillermo or the twins, Maria slipped from bed and met her abuela in the kitchen. There, they shared one cup of black coffee, handing a glazed ceramic mug back and forth, an understanding passing between them that they were different; they were the ones with the don, the gift to heal, and they went to six o'clock Mass each morning to thank Diosito for His gift. Though her abuela advised against being ostentatious with her worship, Maria knelt the whole time on hard tile, enjoying the sharp pain and redness in her kneecaps.

After Mass came the daily lessons on clairaudience—earth-language. Maria learned how to sieve His words from the mundane and decipher them: a grackle's strident cry was a warning, a shriek of caution; a moonless night was a long silence, encouraging Maria to be patient in awaiting changes ahead. She became an interpreter of sorts, known around the neighborhood as Little Vega to distinguish her from her abuela, who was also named Maria. By the time she was grown and her abuela had died, she was simply called Vega.

* * *

Vega was thirty-nine with three kids when she met Miguel Garcia, a married man who came to see her because he suspected he was the victim of brujería. He was weak and fatigued, with soul-numbing migraines, and had twice lost consciousness while operating heavy construction equipment. He'd also lost his appetite and all interest in anything but the military history books he'd collected since his discharge from the Army at twenty-one, right at the end of the Second World War.

"Both times," he said, "right before I fell asleep or fainted, I heard voices. They sounded like children laughing, but there were no children around me. And then it was like I was looking through one of those . . . como se llaman? Those toys that look like binoculars that kids play with?"

"Kaleidoscopes?" Vega suggested.

"Si!" Miguel waved his hands before his eyes. "I saw these zigzags, bright colors. The next thing, I'm opening my eyes. When did I even close them? How much time passed? I was lucky both times. But what if it happens again? When I'm driving? What if I hurt someone?"

Vega sat across from him in the backyard shed she used for consulting clients. They were separated by a small wooden nightstand she had inherited from her abuela. The only light came from a little table lamp, whose linen shade was covered with a burgundy silk handkerchief, and a homemade candle that smelled like spiced vanilla. In the strange combined glow, Miguel's face was wan, his dark eyes feverish in a face chased by shadows.

"And what makes you think it's brujería?" Vega asked.

"I've never been sick. Not even as a child, not even with the flu. This—the children's voices, the visions . . . no." Miguel shook his head. His mustache was thick and still dark, though his sideburns and beard glinted with white. "You'd think that un hombre, a veteran, wouldn't believe in cosas como brujería. But all the things you see when you fight. You lose reason to pretend you can understand everything." He added, "I need my work. Tengo familia, y necesitan comer—can you help me?"

The shed was long and narrow, tight as a jewelry box. On one wall, crimson velvet drapery hung from a shower rod Vega had bought at a garage sale. The other wall was papered with pamphlets and postcards from church: the Virgin Mary, Jesus with outstretched robed arms, patron saints and angels, instructions for how to say the rosary and make confession. An imitation Turkish rug, its sapphire color worn white in some areas, fit the shed from end to end, quieting it. In here was a world not entirely a part of the one outside.

"Let me see your hands," Vega said.

Miguel's work-callused hands looked absurd on the nightstand's lace doily. Vega closed her eyes as she ran her fingertips over the grooves on his palms. The lines that were faint on most people were deep on him, and she felt sweat spring to the surface of his skin. She imagined the sweat as a miniature flood swirling through the dried creekbeds of those grooves, and she lifted his hands to her mouth and pressed her lips against them. She opened her mouth slightly so that he would feel her warm breath, the hint of her tongue.

"Are you crazy?" Miguel asked sharply, pulling away. "What are you doing?"

Vega knew a good, hardworking man when she saw one. Good, hardworking men had fathered her three boys, but, one by one, they'd left and made her start over. She'd looked at Miguel and instantly understood that he was a good provider, a good father, a good husband.

His resistance now was confirmation. She wanted him for her family.

“There is an hechizo against you,” she said. “Somebody has asked a brujo to put a curse on you.”

Miguel’s irritated expression slowly settled into one of crushed wariness: she was the doctor who had just confirmed his worst fear; he was the patient who, while not surprised, still wanted to fight the diagnosis. “Are you sure? How do you know?”

“Your colors tell me. The hechizo is sucking your energy, and everything is faded.” She pointed to a vase that held half a dozen roses, the petals shriveled and dry. “You see those flowers?”

Miguel nodded.

“My son Marcos bought them for me at school. Earlier in the week, they were plump and soft with moisture, full of life. Now they are on the verge of death. The same is true with all of your colors, but your orange . . . ” Vega paused and shook her head, letting her words linger in the air.

“What?” Miguel interrupted. “What about my orange? What is that?”

“It’s the color in your aura indicating protection,” Vega answered. “Where it should be bright and strong, it is almost not there at all. You are vulnerable,” she added softly. “And you can feel it. Can’t you?”

Miguel swallowed once, decisively. “Yes. But why? And who?”

Vega said nothing.

He stared back at her, then at the religious paraphernalia on the wall. "Are you Catholic?"

"Yes."

"I go to Mass every Sunday. I make my confessions. I take communion. I pray." He touched the silk handkerchief covering the lampshade, and for a moment Vega thought he was going to pull it off. But he just rubbed the material between his thumb and forefinger. "And still my 'protection' is almost gone? Still this 'hechizo' stays?"

"Brujería is powerful. Brujos are powerful."

"More powerful than God?"

"It's to do with energy," Vega corrected. "Not faith. I can help you, though—will you let me?"

Miguel sighed and squeezed the back of his neck. He pulled out his wallet. "¿Cuanto me cuesta?"

Vega smiled. "Pay me when you're feeling better."

"No. You've got familia, too." He jerked his chin to the right, where, beyond the crimson drapery and aluminum siding of the shed, a swing set dominated the backyard. "We both have the same needs."

Vega reached for a small sewing pouch she kept beneath her chair. She extracted a pair of cuticle scissors. "For now," she said, "I need you to clip your fingernails."

* * *

Vega's boys were sixteen, twelve, and nine. The oldest she had named Guillermo, after her younger brother, who, at seventeen, had taken the Greyhound to work the oil rigs outside Houston and never been heard from again. The other two were Jose Luis and Marcos, after their fathers. All three had the bright penny-colored eyes of Vega's abuela.

She could hear them trampling through the house as she made dinner. Boys' footsteps, so familiar to her—heavy and clumsy and bursting with machismo; the trail they left of stinking sneakers and dissected insects and heartbreak. She shook her head as she mixed fragrant chopped cilantro into a pan of shredded chicken, onions, and salsa verde. Steam rose, and Vega breathed deeply. Sometime between teaching her about curanderismo and earth-language, her abuela had taught her to cook. For a second, the smell of chicken encilantrada made Vega believe that her abuela was just around the corner, kneeling at her little altar to St. Gabriel, humming a psalm.

The first time Vega had cast an amarre del amor, her abuela had instantly known. Vega was in her early twenties, and the man was a gringo from Arkansas. He had strong freckled arms and a startled laugh and was educated; he was going to become a missionary doctor. Vega imagined boarding airplanes with him, learning new languages. She could practice curanderismo wherever they went, if she needed to. She would bear his children, and eventually they would settle in a large hacienda-style home with a kidney-shaped pool and a fountain where fat orange poi would swim. She saw their life so clearly, almost from the moment they met at the grocery store, that she was surprised when he eventually told her he was leaving in a week and didn't invite her to go with him. So, after her abuela and twin brothers were asleep one night, she prepared a perfume. With mortar and pestle, she ground salt, sandalwood, rose petals, and orange blossom, then added droplets of alcohol to thin the paste. Quietly, she slipped out the back door and into the yard, and she placed the mortar in a little pool of moonlight beneath her bedroom window. Before returning to the house, she gazed at the leaning chain link fence against which her abuela had buried the egg all those years ago; the cement slab that served as a porch with two yellowed plastic lawn chairs; the dozens of clay pots where her abuela grew bergamot and sage, lavender and mint. Vega loved her abuela and her brothers, but she would not miss it here. She wanted more than this, and she did not feel guilty about her desire. Why should she? She listened, closing her eyes. The hot, dry summer breeze, the spirit of everything, agreed: Go, go.

The next night, Vega sequestered herself in the bathroom. She rubbed the perfume behind her ears, on each temple, and against the insides of her knees. She lifted her blouse and pressed it into her naval. Then she remoistened her finger, slipped it beneath her skirt and underwear, and, with a flush of guilty excitement, touched the perfume between her legs. She had a date with the gringo that night.

Her abuela was waiting for her in the hallway. She was in her eighties now but seemed an indeterminate age, lithe and unwrinkled but hunched by osteoporosis. She looked hard at Vega and took the mortar from her hands. "*This* is not what I have taught you," she said, sniffing the perfume. "¿No tienes vergüenza?"

Vega grabbed the perfume back. "I'm not doing anything wrong."

"You're trying to *make* a man love you. No es natural. It is *not* what I taught you."

"Well, maybe you should have. I'm late." She brushed past her abuela and hid the mortar under her bed before leaving the house.

But she did the spell wrong. The gringo left anyway, and when he did, she was pregnant with Guillermo.

"Boys!" she called now, pulling plates from the cabinet. "Come help set the table."

The boys clambered into the kitchen, and Vega shot Jose Luis a reproving look as he muttered, "Faggot," to Marcos. Guillermo rolled his eyes at the younger two, grabbing dishes and clattering them before four of the five seats at the table.

"Watch it with those," Vega said. "They're breakable, you know."

"Yeah, Guillermo," Jose Luis said, tearing paper towels from the roll on the counter. "They're breakable, you know."

Vega sighed. Marcos, the sensitive one, patted her arm. She smiled back at him. "Will you serve the water, amorsito?"

Over the next half hour, as her sons bickered and scraped forks against their plates and rose for second helpings, Vega stared at the empty chair across the table. Boys weren't supposed to grow up without a father. How would they learn how to be men? *Good* men, good husbands and providers? She thought of her brothers: Guillermo, frozen at seventeen with a chipped front tooth and rattail hair; the twins, Samuel and Carlos, now petty thieves and dealers, rough and showing little trace of the children who'd serenely slept on a mattress on the floor. Their abuela had done her best. She'd been a mother when their own mother had refused. But it wasn't enough. That was why Vega had Miguel's fingernail clippings, why she would intensify her own hechizos until he, like the good men before him, fell in love with her and, unlike the good men before him, stayed.

* * *

When Miguel next came to see her, she was wearing perfume. Not one that she made but Chanel No. 5. She'd bought it at one of the tiendas in Nuevo Laredo, where the same items cost half as much as they did a short walk over to this side of the bridge. She reserved the perfume for special occasions—the boys' First Holy Communions and birthday parties, her rare dates—and she loved the heady scent, so perfectly manufactured. It filled the small shed like water, enveloping them, and Vega felt a smug burst of pleasure that Miguel would go home smelling like her skin.

"Tell me about your family," she said to him, cupping one of his hands and spreading it flat with her other, leaving her fingers atop his. He held his hand straight and rigid, not allowing for a single curve of joint that might make their touch feel intimate. "Your wife . . . what's her name?

Miguel's cocoa-colored eyes narrowed. "Por qué?"

Vega's answer was smooth. "You think you're just one man and so the hechizo only affects you. But you are not one man. Once we bind ourselves to someone else through marriage, through children, we cease to be one individual. The hechizo may be against you, but you would be foolish to think it is not also against her. Against your whole family, even. So. What's her name?"

"Sofia," Miguel said, and the syllables of her name thrust the small space into silence. It was as if he'd summoned her, and now her presence felt heavy and accusing.

Vega cleared her throat, angry at the other woman. "And have you noticed her behaving strangely? Anything . . . out of the ordinary?"

Miguel shook his head. "No. Everything is the same as it has been."

"And how is that?" Vega prompted. She smiled at him, a gentle, inviting smile. No teeth. "Tell me, what is your home like? What is the routine? The energy?"

Twin lines formed between Miguel's brows. She waited patiently. He was the kind of man she adored: quiet, each word chosen carefully, reserved and stoic as a soldier. He was the kind of man she wished to crack open, take a chisel to the chest and persistently *thunk, thunk,* thunk it with a mallet until, with a sweet creak, his skin and bone butterflied open before her, everything glistening within, ready for her exploration.

"Sofia and I, we've been married thirty-four years. We are the way people are who know each other well," he said softy. "Sometimes I realize with surprise that we have not spoken in three days, but not in a cold way, an unloving way. Just in the way that happens when you no longer need words like you did when you were younger, when you talked and talked, always trying to get somewhere. Do you know what I mean?"

Vega nodded. "It is much of what I do," she said, though it felt counterintuitive, explaining in words. "Listening to unspoken language."

By the end of their hour together, Vega had learned that his wife, that *Sofia*, was a seamstress, his son in the Marine Corps, and his daughter an English teacher who still lived in the house with her young son. She could tell that Miguel pressured himself to be a father to be the boy, in lieu of his jailed biological one, and could hardly restrain her excited agreement when he said boys needed strong male influences; wasn't that exactly what she thought, too? When footsteps sounded outside the shed, Vega felt shaken from a trance. She had forgotten her next appointment, a regular who came to see her for spiritual consultation. She told Miguel, "Close your eyes." He did, and she prayed for him in Latin, her whisper a soft hiss. Later, she would put an hechizo against his marriage, his peaceful wordless marriage, that it may soon be fractured so that *her* love, *her* boys, could seep into the cracks. Before he even realized it, his dreams, his unspoken words, would be messages to her. Sofia had had him for thirty-four years. Nearly Vega's entire life. It was her turn.

As it happened, though, Miguel was the rarest of good men: his devotion to his family seemed untemptable. The only reason he kept returning to see Vega over the next year, she was certain, was because he worried about the effects his declining health was having on them. He had been let go from his job after again losing consciousness, this time while operating an excavator that was lifting a thousand-pound pipe. The children's voices came on quickly, laughing as his vision filled with those colorful zigzags and his stomach swooped as if he was on a carnival ride. When he opened his eyes, there was a crowd of men yelling below him, surrounding the tractor-trailer where the pipe had crashed. *I'm sorry,* his boss said to him, nearly in tears. *I can't keep you. Por favor, go see the doctors in San Antonio or Houston. Figure out what's wrong.* But of course, without insurance, Miguel could do no such thing. He was stuck seeking handyman jobs, excavators and loaders and dozers replaced by paintbrushes and hammers, children's tools. He was desperate. And the more desperate he became, the more cunning Vega had to be with her hechizos; if he sensed that she was acting in self-interest, even the strongest spells would be futile. So instead of casting amarres del amor, she made him ill in order to cure him; she made him first trust her and then *need* her. And finally, when he was at his weakest, tearfully gaping at the blood that mingled with yolk when she cracked an egg into a glass of water, she kissed him. She kept it short and tender, and he didn't pull away. "I can help you," she whispered. "Will you let me?" He nodded with hollow, deeply sad eyes, and she walked him to her bedroom.

Love. *Could* it be conjured? Yes.

Vega's disappointment after her first failed amarre del amor had made her abuela soften. She'd sat at Vega's bedside and run her ripe, plum-colored fingers across Vega's scalp the way she had when Vega was a girl. "Mijita," she sighed. "This is the most difficult lesson for anybody to learn, and it is especially hard for a curandera—remember the Corinthians? 'If I speak in the tongues of men and of angels, but have not love, I am a noisy gong or a clanging cymbal. And if I have prophetic powers, and understand all mysteries, and all knowledge, and if I have all faith, so as to remove mountains, but have not love, I am nothing.' ¿Recuerdes de eso?"

Vega nodded. How familiar this was, her abuela softly reciting Bible passages, reminding her that healing was a gift and they only vessels. Vega disagreed. A vessel could not guide itself; Vega could.

"So you see, love must be at the center of curanderismo," her abuela continued. "But not in this way. You can open yourself to love and open others to love, and you can help them recover their spirits after losing love, but you cannot control another person's heart. ¿Ahora me entiendes?"

Vega said yes, she did understand, but what she was thinking was that she would learn to do it better.

She knew that the perfume she had made to attract the gringo and the amares del amor she'd cast on the fathers of Jose Luis and Marcos were not part of curanderismo. They were brujería. She knew this, but then, as now, when she sifted inside herself during meditation, she found that she did not care. She deserved happiness. She deserved love. Everyone spoke of selfishness as if it was an evil thing. The most unforgivable of sins, to seek better for oneself, but selfishness was a natural state of being, primal and beautiful. And unlike most people, she had a gift she could use to her advantage; the true sin would be to squander it. Her abuela was wrong. The heart was as vulnerable to energy as the body; the path to it was simply more oblique.

* * *

The woman was young and forgettable the way many gringas were forgettable: straight nutmeg hair, pale eyebrows, skinny, wearing jeans and a t-shirt. She stepped into the shed stooping slightly, as though afraid her head would hit the ceiling. Vega gestured her toward the far chair and took a moment longer than necessary to turn the latch on the shed door. This subtle dramatic action always gave her a sense of power. This was her space, her confessional, her stage. Here, she could invite people into other lives. She could convince them that everything was fluid, no decision irrevocable. Or she could assure them of the infallibility of destiny. They all came to her with their private begging, and she answered the way they needed her to.This was also not what her abuela taught her.

This was also not what her abuela taught her.

They sat across from each other. Vega asked the woman her name.

"Sarah," she said, sounding surprised at the question. "Isn't that something you would just know?"

Vega fought a roll of the eyes; how many times had she been asked that, and always by the gringos? "This must be your first time."

Sarah gave a quick smile and nod. She placed her hands on the table and then removed them, setting them on her lap. Her eyes darted around the shed, and Vega had the sense she could jump up and leave at any moment.

"Perhaps it would help you to know what exactly it is I do," Vega said gently. She lifted the lace doily on the nightstand and retrieved a service menu, which she had typed and Guillermo had had laminated at Office Max. It was a new addition, and it made her feel more like a businesswoman and less like her abuela's version of a curandera, carting yerbas and statuettes and cards across town in plastic bags like a homeless woman. She wondered what her abuela would think about the menu, with bullet point lists under categories like spellwork, spiritual consultation, spiritual cleansing (limpia), card reading, and ritual candle burning.

Sarah went through the menu slowly, flipping pages at the bottom right corner, as though she didn't want to cloud them with her fingerprints.

Her fingernails were creamy and oval-shaped, extending just beyond the pads of her fingers. She was not wearing a wedding ring, Vega noticed, or any jewelry, for that matter.

"My sister," Sarah said softly, still looking at the menu, "has run away. She left everyone she said she loved—her husband, her two girls, our parents and me—without so much as a goodbye. It's been months, and no one has heard from her. A friend of mine comes to see you—Amy?"

Vega nodded. Amy was one of her regulars, an eager young woman in search of some nameless thing, eyes as hopeful as a dog's.

"Anyway," Sarah said, "I just need to know why she left and if she's okay."

Vega nodded. "The worst thing for the spirit is to be left with no answers. But you should know that her reason for leaving and her current state of being are two separate questions, with possibly two very different answers."

Sarah blinked. "Okay," she said, almost defiantly.

"Do you have a photograph of your sister?"

"Oh. I'm—I'm not sure." She leaned down, her fine hair covering her face as she reached for her canvas bag that had dropped on the ground. Vega contained her disapproval. Gringos never seemed to value their possessions. "I'm sorry," Sarah said. "I should have thought . . ." Her hands foraged in the bag until they found her wallet, a long, packed leather pouch that burst open as soon as Sarah touched the button snap. She rifled through receipts, bills, and coins until—"Ah!" She smiled as she slipped a small photo from the mess around it. "It's old, but I have one."

It was a school photo. The girl must've been about fifteen. She wore a pale blue turtleneck sweater, stared into the camera with eyes that the small smile didn't match. Her posture was awkward; she seemed to be sliding down in the seat, her right side lower than her left, though her neck was rigid. Vega looked more closely. The girl's thick hair and turtleneck partly concealed a dark neck brace.

"She was in a wheelchair," Sarah said. "This was after she'd gotten out of the hospital."

"What happened to her?" Vega asked, transfixed and somehow almost shamed by the knowingness in the girl's green eyes.

"Botulism, if you can believe it," Sarah said. "Our mom tried home-canning beets, but she did it wrong, and Genny reacted to the bacteria. She was paralyzed for months and not completely well for more than a year. By that time, people had sort of given up on her." She paused, the color rising to her cheeks. "I didn't. But I guess that doesn't matter to her."

"I see," Vega murmured. "I would like to do a ritual candle burning. But first, may I see your hands?"

Sarah held both hands out to Vega, palms upturned, fingers curved. An offering. Vega ran her fingertips lightly over the lines. She imagined them as a winding racecourse, her fingertip the car, careful on the turns. She waited, eyes shut, for the series of random images she knew would come. It was like the unguarded moments before sleep, when the mind works itself into a frenzy of disjointed pictures, one after the other. She relayed these pictures to clients who listened intently. Vega had found that once an image was implanted in people's minds, they began looking for it in the world. Then, no longer would a certain awning or picnic table or restaurant be just an awning or picnic table or restaurant. It would be transformed into something with meaning. Import. Usually there was no harm in this..But today something was different. The red-velvet theater of Vega's eyelids was blank. Instead, she heard a baby's cry, as stark and wildly alive as if a child were in the room with them. Her eyes flew open and she dropped Sarah's hands.

"What?" Sarah looked down at her palms and then back at Vega. Her gray eyes were wary. "Did you . . . see something?"

"Do you have children?"

Sarah flushed and then paled. "No."

"Are you pregnant?"

"No—I don't think so."

"I'm sorry," Vega said. "May I see your hands again?"

This time, she looked closely at each hand, angling the table lamp to better examine the lines. They were clear and well-formed, largely unbroken—but that baby's cry . . . She closed her eyes and, for the first time in many moonless nights, concentrated the way she had as a girl, when her abuela had taught her about earth-language, about looking not just at blades of grass but at the dirt in between, and the insects in that dirt, and the almost imperceptible tracks they left behind and nearly inaudible sounds they made as they scraped and carried and worked. Now she heard Sarah's breathing, soft and quick; the snap of the candlewick as it burned; the press of wind against the side of the shed. She smelled detergent on Sarah's clothes, dust from the rug and drapery, paper. And the longer she held Sarah's hands, the more she felt the unmistakable sensation of rope being twined around her wrists, tighter and tighter, chafing her skin. She felt a lurch of fear, searing hopelessness. She heard a chorus of women's weeping.

A curandera must hold a deep awareness of others' suffering, her abuela whispered.

"I'm sorry," Vega said, pulling away. "I can't help you."

"What do you mean?" Protectively, Sarah touched her belly. "What did you see? *Am* I pregnant? Is something bad going to happen? What about my sister?"

Vega was shaken, near tears. She could still feel the rope. "Sometimes the answers we find are not the ones we seek. Please, just go."

After a moment, Sarah stood. Her breath was louder now, and she shook her head, a hand still on her abdomen. She looked as though she was about to speak but, on second thought, hurried past Vega toward the door. Vega watched her fumble with the latch, and the shed filled with light as she rushed outside. She didn't look back, and the door swung shut behind her.

Vega held her wrists under the lamp: they were smooth and unmarked. *Espanto*—soul loss—was in Sarah's future. Not just her future, but her daughter's. Vega was certain of these things, and the certainty filled her with frightened awe.

Vega was still sitting on her folding chair when the shed door opened two hours later. The sun had lowered, and the smells of evening and rain startled her from silence. A man stood in the doorway. Vega knew, even in the absence of light, that it was Miguel.

"I've left her," he said. "I've left them all for you."

Vega walked to him and pressed her body against his. He was thin and shaky.

"Come in," she said, taking his hand and pulling him into the shed. "Get undressed while I bring an egg from the house. I think the limpia will work now."

Originally published in our Summer 2017 issue,
Kitchen Table Translation

The Excavation of Identity as a Political Act: A Conversation with Helena Maria Viramontes

Elizabeth Rodriguez Fielder

For nearly four decades, Mexican-American author Helena Maria Viramontes has been telling stories about the issues that are at the forefront for a wider swathe of Americans today: stories of economic inequality and civil rights in marginalized communities. Her stories are rooted in the impact of labor leader and civil rights activist Cesar Chavez, the United Farm Workers Movement, and the Chicano Civil Rights Movement of the 1960s upon her family and community. Her characters, predominantly impoverished women and children, are resilient in their unrelenting love of life and all of humanity. Her writing is indispensable for this new political era of Trump.

Less than one week after the results of the 2016 US Election, writer Elizabeth Rodriguez Fielder interviewed Viramontes for *Sampsonia Way Magazine* and *Aster(ix) Journal.* The two Latinx writers spoke about social movements past and present, families, and the interconnected histories of minorities in the United States in a wide-ranging and revelatory political conversation.

Elizabeth Rodriguez Fielder: We first met on the night of the election at the City of Asylum reading, and now we're meeting again under very different circumstances. For the duration of your career, you've been writing about and defending the very people that are being directly attacked by our president-elect. Now you are here in a place called City of Asylum. If this were in a book no one would believe it! It's almost too poetic to be real. How have you been reflecting and processing that throughout this post-election week?

Helena Maria Viramontes: I just talked to a good friend of mine, Sanjay Mohanty, an incredible colleague at Cornell. I said to him, I couldn't have been in a more perfect place, and I was so grateful to be here exactly at this time of great upheaval and nightmare. I spent so much time on Facebook on Wednesday scrolling and reading posts from the people that were frightened. The one that got to me was this BBC posting of an interview with kids in a third grade classroom. It had to be in Texas. The kids were very outspoken about how they were frightened about their families being torn apart and two or three of them started crying. And that's the only time that I broke. I really broke. I started sobbing myself. Because I've always felt that it's our duty as people who don't have that fear, who have the luxury of not being afraid, to speak up.

There are all these different demonstrations that are going on like, Trump is not my president, and that's good because there's no real message other than the rebellion against the election. But the fact is—I think—they are doing that out of solidarity, out of collectivity. That energy people have when they're together make them less afraid. They become more politically savvy and mobile. Right now, that's just the knee-jerk reaction: go out into the streets. Without any mandates, without any real organization, without looking at the best ways to organize this resistance. But I do feel that's good. Especially the students. Especially "the Dreamers." That collectivity really does feel like something can be done. That my body, that being here, is worth something. That me being here is a good enough protest.

ERF: The current fear can be productive because it's a moment for understanding that there are people that have been experiencing fear regardless of who the president is. Privileged people suddenly feel afraid, creating a chance for empathy with communities that were oppressed before this election.

HMV: One of the reasons I like Facebook is because so many people were responding to the election. And the disbelief and the shock and the fear just went on and on. But several months ago, there was one posting that I do remember that said, *This is exactly why there should be more ethnic studies, courses, more alternative literatures, as part of the mainstream in order to expose, to educate.* How else but literature can you feel that empathy? It's the true power of transformation. Toni Morrison calls it the *dancing of the mind.* Paul Auster says that the most intimate relationship two people can have will be the reader and the writer. Complete and total strangers enter into these particular worlds, the writer's world that the reader has the permission to enter, and complete that act of art.

I think that's one call. For example, as a scholar of these literatures, you are called on to become more vigilant, more assertive, and more argumentative about the necessity of having those courses. Part of the wonderful experience of teaching creative writing is that each course is everything and creative writing. It's an examination of the Self and an examination of each other. It is about morality, politics, character, the senses—these wonderful and beautiful things.

A student in my class had written a story where the character didn't rise to the occasion of being a hero and speaking out. It was about his grandfather, who was next to a concentration camp, his grandfather who was by-and-large silent while living in the occupied communities around the killing camps in Germany. There were several students that objected and said, *This is not historically true, people just didn't know what was going on.* Then I said, *That's very well and true, that could be very historically accurate. Also, this person has the right to write what he or she wants to write.* And I added, *Let's all look at ourselves for a little while here. How many of us would rise to the occasion?* We all think we're going to be the noble people that will rise. But I experienced the 1980's when the AIDS epidemic went on and nobody cared. There were just gay men dying left and right, *who cares?* It moved to drug addicts, then prostitution. *Oh, who cares?* But then it moved into hemophiliacs, and all of a sudden it's like, *Oh my god the innocent!* So I said, *Please don't tell me that we can all rise to the occasion, really think about that.*

ERF: When reading your characters, I see them struggling through a generational gap, linguistically and culturally. As a first-generation American, I find it difficult to connect my own politics with my mother and my extended family. I've sought out role models in different places such as school, but I know a lot of young Latinx people out there who don't have access to the kind of support system I did, and they can face parents with strange political opinions. What is your advice—or perspective–you might offer for young people that are finding it very difficult to talk with their parents at this point in time?

HMV: Wow, that's a big question. From my own experience,my mother was unique. She was born in this country. All of my mother's family was born in this country, except my grandmother and my grandfather who were born in Mexico. And my Tia Andi, who was the oldest of our aunts who died around 1990—she was hitting those nineties—born in 1904—I have her birth certificate. They grew up Americanized, in West Los Angeles, and even though the community was Mexican, they grew up listening to radio shows, being influenced by movies, by things like that. So between 1920 and 1940, they were trying to discover what it was to be American, even though my grandmother and grandfather were Mexican. It was a time that I'm excavating myself in my work because it was such a transition for them.

My mother was different. She was raised Mormon and converted to Catholicism to marry my father. Though she had an altar at the house that my father built which is where I got the inspiration for [my 1995 novel] *Under the Feet of Jesus* because any important paper she literally would put under the feet of Jesus. But she was never somebody who told us that we needed to go to church or imposed Catholicism on us. She had a great belief in God, but she was not of the institutions. Part of it had to do with getting away from the Mormon Church, the other part of it had to do with not agreeing with the Catholic Church, either.

My sisters and I didn't understand how unique they were in their resistance. Whatever my mother's politics, whatever my mother's religion, I saw that she was a creative woman. I acknowledged that not everyone saw what I saw. That was one of my primary inspirations for wanting to write about women, especially the women in my family. My sisters were very rebellious, but only within the confines of their jailed household. My father believed in curfew, in women not going out on dates without chaperones, but my sisters rebelled creatively—and with my mother's help, too! If they would go out with a boy, my mother would be in the kitchen waiting in case my father woke up.

ERF: Yes! When I look at the people surrounding me in my life, I find that I'm not drawing religious or political influence, but rather things like creativity, or a tone of voice that I admire and I can adopt even in a totally different aspect. Many of these moments happen in silence, like watching your mother at the kitchen table. It is a way to potentially connect together across generations despite cultural gaps.

HMV: Right, and in doing that you develop a sense of respect. And you know my mother and sisters were just astounded that they were given these kinds of spaces in my work, honoring and loving, because nobody wrote about them. So I was going to write about them; in a very truthful way, not in a romantic way. And then, because of that development of respect, then you can sit down and have conversations. And that's what I did.

I do have conservative family members, but I have faith in their intelligence. I have a wonderful sister who I respect who is so smart. I realized we couldn't talk politics because I just didn't understand. But then, slowly things would happen, like they just laid off all these people in the company your husband works in, and yet reported a trillion in profits. Because I trust her intelligence, there's a poco that rises up in conversation.

ERF: I feel like we have to be brave to sit down and have a small conversation.

HMV: You begin with small conversations. That's all. You have to trust in people's intelligence, which is what I did with my sisters.

ERF: Your talk of unions warmed my heart, since being a union kid changed my own life. Aside from all the medical benefits, we had cultural discounts that opened doors and a sense of community.

However, the traditional model of the labor movement is shifting and changing today. Obviously, *Under the Feet of Jesus* is taking place at the time of Cesar Chavez and the farmworker's union and you wrote about the hazards of the workers—they do exist today, but in different ways, like in the meat industry and the construction industry. However, we are also seeing the rise of worker centers. How do you see labor today? Do you have hope for the labor movement?

HMV: Yes, I do have hope for the labor movement. Right in the middle of writing *Under the Feet of Jesus,* Cesar Chavez died. So I felt I had to insert him in, and I kept writing these symbolic chapters, about the sun going down as we're walking out into sunset, as tribute to him. But, it didn't click. I wanted to tell Estrella's story, I didn't want to tell mine. And there was a big difference. Working in the fields myself, it was natural that I would be in the United Farm Workers support group. But not for Estrella. So I thought, I'm gonna hold back and not include that. I also didn't want the workers' struggle to take away from the workers, which can happen. I felt it necessary to describe people working. People can talk about sweat, they can talk about the hardships of working in the fields, but to actually see them doing that in a systematic way is something you don't see in literature. So I wrote a whole section about working so people could understand what it takes to pick the grapes.

When *Under the Feet of Jesus* first came out, I was asked by a radio interviewer in one of the New England states, *This novel is about farmworkers, it's about the poor. Can you make an argument for why people should care?*

ERF: Wow.

HMV: Tell me about it. I was taken aback.

ERF: Would you answer, Uh, humanity? The fact that we both have veins with blood coursing through them? The fact that it's arbitrary that you were born in one life, and not in that one?

HMV: It was so strange! Well all I can say is, have you eaten an apple today? Are you going to have a salad for lunch? Are there buffets where you can pick your vegetables? Are you going to have string beans for dinner? And I said, and who do you think picks those? Every one of the vegetables and fruit I mentioned has the handprints of farmworkers. And that's why you should care. I was so astounded but it woke me up too. Not everyone's going to understand that.

ERF: Do you see that lack of understanding as a part of our society and our culture–especially at a level of privilege—where people are very distanced from even the process of growing things? In some ways I see it as a conduit to activism, to understanding the processes that go in and supporting in some way the environmentalist movement's call for local and small scale.

HMV: Absolutely. In fact David Vasquez and Sarah Wall interviewed me for a book on ecocriticism. Part of what they're talking about is the divorcing of the food systems, so that agribusiness can come in and do whatever the *fuck* they want. So you have these horrible slaughterhouses that Wall writes about or that *Fast Food Nation* writes about. What I like about Sarah Wall's work is that she takes to task the author of *Fast Food Nation* [Eric Schlosser], who describes these the chaotic, filthy industry but overlooks the mejicanos doing the work. In her argument, she's saying, he's concerned about the cruelty toward the animals, but what about the cruelty toward the workers?

ERF: The cruelty to the workers is the reason why I'm vegetarian. It gives me an opportunity to speak about the people being exploited in the factories. That could have been me if I was born under a different set of circumstances.

HMV: It is serendipitous. That's the scary part about these lives of ours. I almost dropped out when I was in the eighth grade. Both my sister Frances–a year and a half above me–and I stopped going to school. So my mother—knowing that my sister was out in the streets—stayed home. But she had us cleaning left and right. And after about a couple of weeks I thought, man I don't want to do this! Maybe I'll go back. And my sister did end up dropping out and she did end up cleaning houses. Until my mother–see she was very Americanized–found a job course and they had programs for at-risk youth and so she sent Frances there and Frances was able to work as a nurse's aid and then get a nursing degree. If I had dropped out, who knows? If it wasn't for a drama teacher who I just loved…and I loved drama. So I went to Garfield and I pursued that. I even wrote a play. Who knows what happened to it, but that saved me.

ERF: Theater becomes a way of allowing people that normally wouldn't, to come together. Since your reading at City of Asylum, I've been thinking about Filipinos, who were involved in the migrant workers struggle and even performed on the picket lines with them in El Teatro Campesino's plays. There are so many groups on the border of Chicana/o and Latinx identities, right?

HMV: Right, just like these Punjabi workers! The more I do research on it for my book, the more I see the parallels.

ERF: Could you talk about how those parallels could be mobilized within the movement? How might different ethnic groups be able to come together in a productive way?

HMV: I don't want to be a reductionist, certainly not an essentialist. I was doing research for this book in South Central in L.A., where the neighborhood had completely transformed from African American to Central American and you can barely see the traces. You see a little sign that says, *South Central was once the jazz quarter of the world*, and that's it. Just like on Chavez' grave, they have a little pot of flowers and that's it. It's dismissed, it's buried. Fast-forward to a couple of years later, when I'm invited by USC along with Dana Johnson and Héctor Tobar to talk about race. It was a writerly panel for writers who write about race, but it was publicized differently and the place was packed with at least 200 people, most of them teachers and students and professors. After we each did our presentation, there was a Black woman who got up and said, *I brought my students here, this was very disappointing. I thought we were really gonna talk about race.* She said, *Do you realize how violent it has been in the high schools? Where there's been Latinx and Black violence time and time again?* So I thought maybe we could really have conversations like that. I just said, *We're gonna really have to think about vocabulary to start these conversations.*

If we know each other's history, we will be able to see parallels in this history. If the Black students knew about the Jazz Quarter and the incredible historic events, I bet they would feel a certain pride. And the Central Americans would understand that there was a transformation and maybe have a little respect. Perhaps then there would maybe be more conversation between them. But if we don't find those parallels, there's going to be an incredible war.

ERF: Absolutely, and that must be a lot of pressure for you as an author when you sit down to write. To try to encompass all of these different backstories, and these different histories, in order to create those parallels in your work. But how are you handling the stress of that?

HMV: It's very stressful, and the worst thing that anybody could tell me is that I'm writing a stereotype, or that this is just expository. It's a real challenge, and yet there is beauty in exploring these types of lives. I have this Punjabi character who meets a Mexican woman in El Centro, and they're going to get married. In California, it wasn't legal to have interracial marriage. So they have to go to Gallup, New Mexico on a segregated train in 1935. In the "Coloreds Only" compartment, he looks at a Black woman with a headwrap and he smiles because he's wearing his turban. And she smiles, creating a little moment. As they're traveling, he starts to reflect and understand segregation because of colonized British India. Many of the Punjabi men were actually military men that were under the British Indian Army because they were known as warriors. They have lion hearts. I imagine he's part of the British Indian Army of which 65 percent of the men came from Punjab. The whole battalion went to suppress a revolt against the British in which the Shi'ites and the Sunnis joined together. So here is a British colonial Indian fighting to suppress liberty. Then he has an epiphany. He experiences the harm and the trauma of war, but it's in a different body. It's not a U.S. service man, it's a Punjabi man. Then he meets this Mexican woman. You see what I mean? It's like, *oh, this is crazy!*

ERF: Do you feel that this novel you're writing is a global novel?

HMV: It sort of is but it isn't, because there are only these little instances, but it's also pulling together those parallels, it's interweaving those stories, it's showing that–at least if I do this right–that we can have a Punjabi man parallel a U.S. serviceman in the type of haunting that happened during World War II. So he comes back with post-traumatic stress syndrome and all he does is work the fields, and he meets a housekeeper who has just lost her husband, they decide to get married. It's all because he comes to California, all because of the war, this epiphany about liberation and the fact that he's not liberated, and yet he's fighting for the very power that colonized him and his people.

ERF: Those parallels are powerful. Especially with undocumented workers and the larger history of human migration. Their stories create parallels to open people's minds so that they can understand that experiences are connected. The work of empathy is so hard. Aren't we built to naturally have empathy for each other in order to survive?

HMV: But you know we live in a society that has certain rules, like white is right. These are dominant, patriarchal, and sexist-enforced rules. How could the U.S. annex the Southwest, where suddenly Mexico becomes the U.S., and citizens lose their land? It was so easy for them. All they said was that you don't have the legal documents. This is what we do in the U.S.

ERF: Another arbitrary circumstance.

HMV: Greed and manipulation has existed throughout the history of the U.S., including with the colonization of the Philippines. The Philippines and the U.S. were allies against the Spanish. And as soon as that happened, they were independent for like two years. And then the U.S. decided they wanted to have them, and that was it. So of course they fought them, but they were no match and so they became possessions of the U.S. Look at Puerto Rico. It's incredible. There are all these other places that they've grabbed for resources.

ERF: Narratives and stories are able to encompass both the historical knowledge and the strange affinities with the different characters. Authors can create moments where people can meet outsiders and understand that identity is something that's flexible, that can change moment to moment as well.

HMV: As long as you understand your basic cores and principles of who you are. I can see that flexibility, but my basic cores are always about human rights, always speaking up for those who can't, always recognizing when to speak up and how to do it. I try to do this through my writing. Going back and looking at these parallels, it's fascinating. And also, I'm trying to give little history lessons too. I'm trying to create a historical narrative that is dramatic.

ERF: On the reverse, scholars and historians should tell personal stories of the people they study and research as well. Identity is a touchy issue that causes high levels of tension. A lot of the characters you write, such as Ben Brady and Turtle from [your 2007 novel] *Their Dogs Came With Them*, express the anxiety of walking within multiple identity categories. How do we quiet and calm the anxiety of identity?

HMV: Nobody has the degrees, the historical context, to tell you you're not someone that you think you are. Nobody has that right. As Malcolm X said, you're going to call yourself something different than what somebody else calls you. I no longer waste my time when people question my identity, because I know who I am. I know what I stand for. And I know what I work for. I say, *Don't you dare question me on that particular thing. On everything else you can, I'm very open, but not for that.*

ERF: I group those people in the same category as those who assume I like spicy food. I have a final question from a student in my class who read [your 1985 short story collection] *The Moths and Other Stories.* He writes:

> *"The symbolism of a moth associated with the death of a family member is relating a very dark, inconceivable moment of pain with the moth's ability to navigate and survive the dark without ever being recognized for its beauty, much like the grief of death can blind the living from the beautiful moment of passing that ends suffering and anguish. Is the story meant to give the reader the mystical, otherworldly feeling about death (like reincarnation for example) or is it simply meant to help people on this earth understand and cope with death?"*

HMV: That is beautiful! I wrote that story when I was 23, 24 years old. It was the only time that I wrote a story in about two weeks. I have never done anything like that again. I'm a constant reviser. The story was in tribute to this pregnant woman who was working in the fields with the sprays, pesticides, and found out that the sprays had deformed her child. I was inspired by a photograph of a Japanese woman who was bathing her badly deformed child. What was so touching to me was the loving gaze that she had for her daughter. And, that the daughter had for the mother. Even though she was deformed, there was this brilliance of illuminating light. And I said, I want to write about that. That's what motivated me to end the story in the bathtub. Now that I'm past 60, I've had a number of different deaths in the family, some that were tragic, some that I was there for, a part of. I've come to realize that in those moments, there is that imbrication, there is that layering between the living and the dying. It is a special mystical moment. And I realize that I had written about it forty years earlier with *The Moths.* I don't know how many people told me that when they read that, they really grieve for their grandmothers, they grieve for their mothers, they grieve for their children.

ERF: One of my students said the same exact thing. It made him miss and grieve his abuelita. The mystical becomes a real thing that helps a person cope.

HMV: Exactly. And the only time it seems to me, is when you're helping the dying. You're being pulled into the death, but at the same time there's no way you can join them, no matter how much you love this person. There is that imbrication. It's very powerful and because there was such a sense of love that this story came out of, I got something right about imbrication. And now that I've experienced it, I know I got it right.

-

Editors' note: this interview has been condensed and edited for clarity. The entire original conversation is available to read online.

Contributor Bios & Acknowedgments

Kianny N. Antigua is a Senior Lecturer of Spanish at Dartmouth College, and an independent translator and adapter for Pepsqually VO Sound & Design, Inc. Antigua has published twenty-four books of children's literature (seven by commission), five of short stories, two collections of poems, an anthology in two languages, a book of microfiction, and a novel. She has won sixteen literary awards and many of her texts have been included in anthologies, literary journals, newspapers and textbooks. Some have been translated into English, French and Italian. She is the translator (Eng./Spa.) and the audiobook narrator of *Dominicana* (Seven Stories Press, 2021), by Angie Cruz; translator of the children's novel *Lucky Broken Girl,* by Ruth Behar; the YA novel *Never Look Back* (Bloomsbury/Audible, 2022), by Lilliam Rivera; and the picture book *Plantains Go with Everything* (HarperCollins, 2023), by Lissette J. Norman.

Fiona Cheong is the author of *The Scent of the Gods* (W.W. Norton, 1991) and *Shadow Theatre* (Soho, 2002). Her shorter work can be found in *Charlie Chan is Dead: An Anthology of Contemporary Asian American Literature* and *Tilting the Continent: Southeast Asian American Writing.*

Sandra Cisneros has won multiple awards, fellowships, and honors as an internationally recognized writer. On September 22, 2016, President Barack Obama presented Cisneros with the National Medal of Arts for her work. Her book called *The House on Mango Street*, has sold over six million copies and has been translated into over twenty languages.

Edwidge Danticat is an award-winning novelist and short story writer, known for her work on national identity, mother-daughter relationships, and diasporic politics. Born to Haitian parents, Danticat was raised by an aunt and uncle in Haiti until she was 12 years old, when she immigrated to New York to join her parents. After a childhood steeped in storytelling and literature, she published her first novel, *Breath, Eyes, Memory* in her early twenties to critical acclaim. She has published over a dozen novels, as well as written several short stories and films.

Katrina Dodson is the translator of *The Complete Stories,* by Clarice Lispector (New Directions, 2015), winner of the PEN Translation Prize and other awards. Her translation of Mário de Andrade's 1928 Brazilian modernist classic, *Macunaíma: The Hero With No Character* will be published by New Directions in 2023. She is currently adapting her Lispector translation journal into a book, and her writing has appeared in *The Paris Review, The Believer, McSweeney's, Triple Canopy* and elsewhere. Dodson holds a PhD in Comparative Literature from the University of California, Berkeley and is an affiliated scholar of the Brazil LAB at Princeton University. A San Francisco native, she now lives in Brooklyn and teaches translation at Columbia University.

Yalitza Ferreras is the 2022 - 2023 Carol Houck Smith Fiction Fellow at the University of Wisconsin's Institute for Creative Writing in Madison, WI. She is the recipient of a 2020 Rona Jaffe Foundation Writers' Award and a recent Steinbeck Fellow at San Jose State University. Her writing has appeared or is forthcoming in *Best American Short Stories, Kenyon Review, Bellevue Literary Review, The Southern Review,* and elsewhere.

Katie Gutierrez is the author of the national bestselling and Edgar-nominated debut novel *More Than You'll Ever Know,* which was also a Good Morning America Book Club selection. She is a National Magazine Award finalist whose writing has appeared in *TIME, Harper's Bazaar, Longreads,* and more. She has an MFA from Texas State University and lives in San Antonio, Texas, with her husband and their two kids.

Nathalie Handal is described as a "contemporary Orpheus." She is the author and/or editor of 10 award winning books, including *Life in a Country Album*, winner of the Palestine Book Award; the flash collection The Republics, lauded as "one of the most inventive books by one of today's most diverse writers," and winner of the Virginia Faulkner Award for Excellence in Writing and the Arab American Book Award. Her nonfiction has appeared in *Vanity Fair, Guernica, The Guardian, The New York Times, The Nation,* and *The Irish Times*, among others. Handal is the recipient of awards from the PEN Foundation, the Lannan Foundation, Fondazione di Venezia, Centro Andaluz de las Letras, and the Africa Institute, among others. She is professor at New York University, and writes the literary travel column, "The City and the Writer" for *Words without Borders* magazine.

Mubanga Kalimamukwento is a Zambian storyteller. She has an MFA from Hamline University, an LL.M. from the University of Minnesota (twin cities) and an LL.B. from Cavendish University Zambia. Until 2019, she practised law in Zambia. She is the author of *The Mourning Bird* (Jacana Media) and *unmarked graves* (Tusculum University Press). She is the winner of the Dinaane Debut Fiction Award (2019), the Kalemba

Short Story Prize (2019), the Writer of Color Merit Scholarship (2020 - 2023), the Deborah Keenan Poetry Scholarship (2021), the Jacobson Scholarship (2021) and the Tusculum Review Poetry Chapbook Prize (2022). Her work has appeared on Brittle Paper's Top 15 Debut Books of 2019 and shortlists for the; Commonwealth Short Story Prize, Raz-Shumaker Book Prize, Minnesota Author Project, Bristol Short Story Prize, Nobrow Short Story Prize, Bush Fellowship, Miles Morland Scholarship, & Rolex Mentor and Protégé Arts Initiative. She's been anthologized on Netflix and in various journals, including *adda* and *Overland*. When she isn't writing, Mubanga works as the fiction editor at *Doek!* and a mentor at the Minnesota Prison Writing Workshop.

Madhu Kaza was born in Andhra Pradesh, India and grew up in Detroit, Michigan. She is currently an educator, writer and artist based in New York. Much of her work is informed by her astonishment at everyday life.

Jessica Lanay is a poet and short story writer originally from the Florida Keys. She is interested in writing towards the incalculable nature of human emotions, psychology and metaphysical dilemmas. She holds an MFA in Poetry at the University of Pittsburgh where she worked with the Center for African American Poetry and Poetics. She is a Cave Canem and Callaloo fellow; she has workshopped with poets such as Carl Hancock Rux, Gregory Pardlo, Evie Shockley, and Lyrae Van Clief-Stefanon. She also founded a women's editorial group called The Jasper Collective while working in the advertising department of *Poets & Writers Magazine*. It was during her work with the Jasper Collective that she had her first publishing successes. She believes that working with a diverse body of women in editorial partnership was a large reason for achieving those publications. Jessica Lanay's writing can be found in *Five Quarterly, Crab Fat Literary Magazine, TAYO Literary*

Journal, Tahoma Literary Review, Duende, and *Black Candies: A Journal of Literary Horror* and others. She is currently working on a collection of poetry and a short story collection.

Melissa Lozada-Oliva is a poet & educator living in Brooklyn by way of Boston. She is the author of chapbooks *rude girl is lonely girl!* & *peluda*. Her work has been featured in *Remezcla, Buzzfeed, Glamour Magazine, Muzzle, Bustle, Huffington Post,* & *The Guardian*. She is currently an MFA candidate at NYU's Graduate Program for Creative Writing.

Keya Mitra is the author of the novel manuscript, *Love After Life*, as well as *Human Enough*, a finalist for the 2021 PEN/Bellwether Prize for Socially Engaged Fiction. She has completed three novels—*Human Enough, Dead and Married*, and *My Surrogate* (a semifinalist for the Amazon Breakthrough Novel Contest)—a book-length memoir, and a short-story collection that has been a finalist for the Bakeless Prize, the Flannery O'Connor Short Fiction Award, the Mary McCarthy Prize in Short Fiction, and the Dzanc Diverse Voices Prize, and a semifinalist for the Iowa Short Fiction Award. In 2022, she earned a $10,000 prestigious Arnold L. Graves and Lois S. Graves Award in the Humanities, given every two years, for "outstanding teaching in the Humanities" to research her novel *Immigrant Delay Disease* in Meghalaya, India. She is also at work at a novel-in-progress: *Bad Babies*. A Fulbright Scholar and graduate (PhD and MFA) of the University of Houston's creative writing program, Keya is Director of Creative Writing and Editing and Publishing, Associate Professor of Literature and Creative Writing, and Co-Editor-in-Chief of the internationally distributed literary magazine, *Silk Road Review: A Literary Crossroads,* at Pacific University, where she was awarded the 2018 President's Award for Excellence in Teaching.

VI KHI NAO is the author of seven poetry collections & of the short stories collection, *A Brief Alphabet of Torture* (winner of the 2016 FC2's Ronald Sukenick Innovative Fiction Prize), the novel, Swimming with Dead Stars. Her poetry collection, *The Old Philosopher,* won the Nightboat Books Prize for Poetry in 2014. Her book, *Suicide: the Autoimmune Disorder of the Psyche* will be out of 11:11 in Spring 2023. A recipient of the 2022 Jim Duggins, PhD Outstanding Mid-Career Novelist Prize, her work includes poetry, fiction, film and cross-genre collaboration. She was the Fall 2019 fellow at the Black Mountain Institute: https://www.vikhinao.com

Cecca Austin Ochoa is a queer fiction writer of Salvadoran descent. Her fiction has appeared in *Art XX, MAKE: Literary Magazine, Nat. Brut, Anthologized in Pariahs* (SFA Press) and forthcoming in *IMANIMAN* (Aunt Lute Press). Cecca serves as Managing Editor for *Apogee Journal.* She is a 2014 Alumnus of Voices of Our Nation's Artists. In 2011, she received the Astraea Foundation's Lesbian Writers Award. She is currently at work on her first novel Desaparecida about a young woman adopted during the Civil War in El Salvador and raised in the United States.

Celeste Prince, originally from Colorado, graduated from the University of Houston's MFA fiction program in 2013. In the past, she has attended the Callaloo Writers' Workshop and the Sewanee Writers' Conference, as well as taught creative writing to middle and high school students. Currently she lives with her cat in St. Louis, MO, teaching high school English.

Ivelisse Rodriguez's debut short story collection *Love War Stories* was a 2019 PEN/Faulkner finalist and a 2018 Foreword Reviews INDIES finalist. It was noted as a must read or best book of the year in over thirty publications, including *O magazine, Women's Health, Good Housekeeping, Cosmopolitan,* and more. She is a contributing arts editor for the *Boston Review*, where she acquires fiction. She is a 2022 Letras Boricuas fellow, a Tanne Foundation award winner, a Kimbilio fellow, and a VONA/Voices alum. She earned an M.F.A. in creative writing from Emerson College and a Ph.D. in English-creative writing from the University of Illinois at Chicago.

Elizabeth Rodriguez Fielder is a scholar of twentieth and twenty-first century transnational American literature and culture. Her teaching and research interests include multiethnic literature and culture, (specifically African American and Latinx Studies), performance studies, women of color feminism, southern studies, and social movement activism. She received her PhD from University of Mississippi in English; an MA in American Studies from Columbia University; and a BA in English/ Creative Writing from SUNY Binghamton. Her book project "Cultural Activism and the Civil Rights Movement" is a multidisciplinary study of creative activism and performance by minority artists and revolutionaries in the 1960s and 70s. This book engages in the role of creativity in social movements and argues that the aesthetics of cultural production shaped civil rights politics. Rodriguez Fielder presents a vision of social movement activism where the collaborative production of performances and of experimental media overlapped with quotidian activities, such as farming okra and sewing quilts. Her work has appeared in *The Global South, The Cambridge History of the Literature of the U.S. South, PMLA, Undead Souths, Fifty Years After Faulkner,* and *Tropical Gothic* with topic ranging from radicalism in Florida to ghosts in Faulkner.

Sejal Shah is a queer brown neurodiverse writer of Kenyan, Ugandan, Indian, Gujarati, and American background. She is the author of the essay collection *This Is One Way to Dance* (University of Georgia Press), an NPR Best Book of 2020. "The Girl With Two Brothers" is the opening story of her forthcoming book, *How to Make Your Mother Cry: fictions* (West Virginia University Press, 2024). She lives and writes in Western New York.

Helena María Viramontes is the author of *The Moths and Other Stories* and two novels *Under the Feet of Jesus* and *Their Dogs Came With Them.* She has also co-edited with Maria Herrera Sobek, two collections: *Chicana (W) rites: On Word and Film* and *Chicana Creativity and Criticism.* A recipient of numerous awards and honors, including the John Dos Passos Award for Literature, and a United States Artist Fellowship, her short stories and essays have been widely anthologized and her writings have been adopted for classroom use and university study. Her work is the subject of a critical reader titled *Rebozos De Palabras* edited by Gabrielle Gutierrez y Muhs and published by the University of Arizona Press. A community organizer and former coordinator of the Los Angeles Latino Writers Association, she is a frequent reader and lecturer in the U.S. and internationally. Currently she is completing a draft of her third novel, *The Cemetery Boys.*

Acknowledgments

"Still Life" by Cecca Austin Ochoa was originally published online in June 2016 with Kweli, a digital-only journal whose mission is to nurture emerging writers of color and create opportunities for their voices to be recognized and valued. Aster(ix) partnered with Kweli for our Spring 2017 issue to help preserve some of those works in print.

"Unfading" by Nathalie Handal was part of a collection of micro-pieces commissioned by Angie Cruz in response to Cecilia Vicuña's painting 1972 "Amaranta" which was "lost and reborn" when found in 2021.

"Love Story for a Foreign Girl" by Fiona Cheong was first published online by *Eastlit.*

"The Girl With Two Brothers" by Sejal Shah was previously published in *Denver Quarterly* in 2010.

"Dalila" by Kianny Antigua was translated by Noah T. Myers for our 2014 issue, a special edition to feature Kianny's work. The Spanish version previously published in *El tragaluz del sótano, Cuentos,* Artepoética Press.

"Summe of Nene" by Ivelisse Rodriguez was originally published by *Boston Review* in 2005.

"House Call" by Melissa Lozada-Oliva first appeared in Muzzle Magazine and also appears in Peluda (Button Poetry, 2017).

If you enjoyed this issue of *Aster(ix)*
and want to share or see more of our work,
please visit www.asterixjournal.com
or scan the QR code below:

@asterixjournal

www.ingramcontent.com/pod-product-compliance
Lightning Source LLC
Chambersburg PA
CBHW061433210726
48287CB00007B/2195

* 9 7 8 1 9 4 2 5 4 7 2 1 1 *